Books by E. X. Ferrars

DANGER
from the
DEAD

DOUBLEDAY

New York
London
Toronto
Sydney
Auckland

DANGER
from the
DEAD

E. X. FERRARS

M
Ferrars

3/93
16.50

A Perfect Crime Book
PUBLISHED BY DOUBLEDAY
a division of Bantam Doubleday Dell Publishing Group, Inc.
666 Fifth Avenue, New York, New York 10103
DOUBLEDAY is a trademark of Doubleday, a division
of Bantam Doubleday Dell Publishing Group, Inc.

Library of Congress Cataloging-in-Publication Data
Ferrars, E. X.
    Danger from the dead / E. X. Ferrars.
        p.   cm.
    I. Title.
PR6003.R458D36   1992   91-26216
823'.912—dc20   CIP
ISBN 0-385-41995-3

DANGER
from the
DEAD

CHAPTER 1

The cottage which Nigel Cleaver had offered to his brother
Gavin for the six weeks of the summer holidays was near
the village of Upthorn, which was in a fold of the Oxford-
shire downs, near to the town of Tolcaster. Gavin had
stayed at Upthorn before and thought it pleasant, but the
idea of spending August and some of September there
would not have filled him with enthusiasm but for two
things.

One was that another plan that he had made to go on a
Hellenic cruise with a friend had fallen through, due to the
friend having got married rather suddenly. Gavin could
still have gone on the cruise by himself, but the thought
of plunging alone among a number of strangers, perhaps
venturing on being friendly with some of them, or else staying carefully in his own shell, both seemed unattractive.
Gavin in middle age was as shy as he had been all his life,
though necessity had made him learn to conceal it more
successfully than he had when he was younger. A school-
master in even a relatively minor public school like Stillborough, where Gavin had taught history for ten years,
cannot afford to let the boys in his charge know how vulner-
able he is to their opinion of him, how much he shrinks
from their possible scorn or dislike. In fact, he had always
been fairly popular with them and he knew this, but to
maintain his position was a constant strain which made the
school holidays, especially the long weeks in the summer,
as welcome to him as they were to the boys. He had really
looked forward to that cruise. The cottage at Upthorn
would not be much of a compensation for having had to

abandon it except for the second thing that Nigel had mentioned when he made his offer.

This was that his sister-in-law, Caroline, was staying with him and his wife Annabel, who had had a stroke two years before and ever since had been a semi-invalid. Gavin had once thought himself in love with Caroline and the thought of being near her for a few weeks stirred greater excitement in him than he would have expected. He was only half aware of this. If he had understood himself more fully he would very likely have refused Nigel's invitation, pressing as it had been. Oddly pressing, Gavin started to think soon after he had accepted it. Nigel had seldom gone out of his way to show Gavin any particular friendliness, even if he had never shown him the hostility that he did to his two sisters. But he had certainly been very emphatic that having Gavin for a time as a neighbour in that cottage in the downs would please him immensely, and if the oddity of it had not gradually made Gavin uneasy, the thought of this would have pleased him too, because he had always felt what he believed was an altogether unappreciated admiration of his older brother.

However, he was not thinking much about this when he arrived at the cottage on the Friday morning after the school had broken up. He had driven about ninety miles from Stillborough and it was twelve o'clock when he reached Upthorn. The cottage was about a mile from the village down a narrow, winding lane, and had once been the stables and carriage-house of the old stone house where Nigel and Annabel lived. But they had converted the barn into an independent cottage, had furnished it and usually rented it to someone who happened to want a few months of quiet in the country, or else might be working in Tolcaster but had not yet found an adequately desirable house or flat there.

Why they had done this Gavin did not know, for they

did not need the money. But he supposed that to see the unused stables gradually disintegrating into a ruin had irked them, while to have re-thatched the roof and painted the rotting doors merely for appearance's sake might have seemed an irritating expense. Between the two buildings there was a wide gravelled courtyard with an oval rose-bed in the centre.

When Gavin arrived the gate into the courtyard stood open and he drove first to Nigel's house to obtain the key to the cottage and to find out if there were any special instructions for him in his use of it. Stopping his car at the door of the big house, he got out and went up to the heavy oak front door and rapped on it with the black iron knocker.

Gavin at forty was of medium height and slight of build though with broad, slightly stooping shoulders, and a face that was thin and nervous, with hollow cheeks and a high forehead already marked with wrinkles which would have made him look still older than he was if it had not been for his wide grey eyes which seemed to survey the world with a bright, interested and almost innocent youthfulness. His hair was light brown, receding a little above the temples, and was usually somewhat shaggy. He was not aware of being a good-looking man, his idea of what good looks ought to be in a man having been imprinted on his imagination in his boyhood by his brother Nigel, but more people than he realized found him attractive. If he had realized it he would probably not have known what to do about it.

When he had knocked at the door a second time and still received no answer, he returned to his car and drove it round the courtyard to the door of the cottage.

It was two storeys high, was painted white with a few dark beams showing through the plasterwork, had four small windows overlooking the courtyard, a door painted pale green and a steep roof of thatch over what had once been a hay-loft, but now contained two bedrooms and a bathroom.

As Gavin stopped the car, wondering if the door would be unlocked so that he could go in, it was thrown open and a very small woman came out to meet him.

'You'll be Mr Cleaver's brother,' she stated. 'I said I'd stay here to meet you in case he wasn't home in time.'

She looked about fifty and was very slim as well as short, with small, neat features in a pointed little face. She was wearing dark blue trousers and a brilliantly patterned shirt and had a bunch of fair curls tied with a scarlet ribbon in a clump on top of her head.

'My name's Mrs Nevin,' she said. 'You can call me Beatie if you like. Or Beatrice. I come in here to clean Tuesdays and Fridays. I hope that'll suit you.'

Gavin thought that he would opt for Beatrice, though he would really have preferred to call her Mrs Nevin, the habit of being on instant Christian name terms with complete strangers being one which he still found difficult to accept. But he was afraid that she might resent so much formality.

'Of course it'll suit me splendidly,' he said as he once more got out of the car and opened the boot to extract his suitcase. 'I tried knocking at the other house but there wasn't any answer.'

'That's right,' she said. 'Mrs Cleaver never comes to the door. She's so slow with her stick, she's given up trying to do it. And Mr Cleaver can't have got back from his work yet, but he'll soon be home for lunch. Always comes home for his lunch unless there's something special keeps him in Tolcaster. But he told me particularly he'd be home today because of you arriving. I don't normally stay as late as this, I comes from nine to eleven, but I said I didn't mind for once. Your bed's made and towels in the bathroom and everything, and there's things for your lunch in the fridge.'

She turned and stepped back into the cottage, the curls

on top of her head bobbing as she went and her thin little body moving as lightly as that of a young girl.

Gavin, carrying his suitcase, followed her. The door opened straight into the living-room of the cottage. The room was bigger than might have been expected from outside, for it occupied almost the whole of the ground floor. Two doors opened out of it, one into the tiny though well-arranged kitchen, and the other, which looked more like the door of a cupboard than one that led anywhere, actually opened on to a narrow, steep staircase. The floor was of old red tiles with a square of rather shabby carpet in the centre, some shabby though sufficiently comfortable Victorian furniture, and some flower prints on the walls, which were painted pale pink and had an electric fire let into one of them. Gavin remembered that Annabel had had a Victorian period which had coincided with some bestsellers that she had written about young ladies in crinolines and gentlemen with whiskers, but growing tired of it, no doubt, had used all the odds and ends that had not been valuable enough to sell to furnish the cottage. The result, in its way, was homely and pleasant. The one window looked straight across the courtyard to the stone house opposite.

'Isn't Miss Astor staying here?' he asked. 'Mrs Cleaver's sister.'

'That's right,' she said. 'But not knowing when you'd be arriving and having some shopping to do in the village, I expect she's gone out. She's been here ever since Mrs Gates left. She was housekeeper here after Mrs Jameson left, who was housekeeper after Miss Meldrum. I don't know where they'd be without Miss Astor now. Poor Mrs Cleaver's wonderful really, she's so brave and she still writes her books, but she can't do all that much for herself.'

'Why such a succession of housekeepers?' Gavin asked. 'Don't they like it here?'

'Well, it's kind of lonely, isn't it?' the little woman said.

'It's a good mile to the village and very quiet at nights. I live in the village myself and I come on my bicycle, and I've been coming ever since Mr and Mrs Cleaver moved in, which is twelve years ago now, and it suits me, but then I don't want all my neighbours watching everything I do and talking about it. There's no one near here but Dr and Mrs Jay in that house you passed just before you got here. You may have noticed it. They're nice people, quiet, and they don't bother you. And then I've always got on very well with Mrs Cleaver. You know her, so you'll know it isn't everyone does. She's sometimes got a funny way of putting things, as if you wasn't quite good enough for her. But I know she doesn't mean any harm and I never takes any notice. I just gets on with my work and she leaves me alone, which is how I like it.'

Gavin did know Annabel and knew that she did indeed have a funny way of putting things, as if hardly anyone was quite good enough for her. He did not think that she knew that she had this effect on people, for usually she seemed to make a considerable effort to charm them. Perhaps the trouble was that the effort was too apparent. It was always important to her to be the centre of attraction in any gathering in which she found herself, and beginning with a husband who was ten years younger than herself and continuing with friends and so probably also to housekeepers, this could seem more like patronage than real good nature.

She must have been very beautiful when she was young, Gavin had always thought, for she had still had most of that beauty when he had first met her with Nigel, when she had already been forty. Now, even at sixty and since her stroke slightly crippled, some of it remained. She had aston-ishing eyes, large and a brilliant blue, set in an oval face with strong yet delicately modelled features, and a body which only since her illness had become heavy. Before that, as he remembered it, it had had a certain solidity, but had had a gracious and dignified poise, with something about it that suggested warm sensuality. Her hair now, Gavin believed, was white, though she denied this and insisted that its pale gold was natural and not a skilful tint job. She was not the most truthful of women and usually took at least seven years off what he happened to know was her age, so a false claim about her hair was not unlikely. Though this characteristic of hers mildly irritated him, he had a good deal of admiration for her, even if he could not read the books that she wrote.

Most of them were historical romances, and as a teacher of history himself he had to admit that there was nothing lacking in the carefulness of her research, but he had not much romance in his nature and after he had tried, out of regard for Nigel, to read two or three of them, he had decided not to pretend that he found them compulsive reading, which, luckily for her and for Nigel, a great many people did. She had accepted this in Gavin with a touch of the sardonic humour of which she was occasionally capable and which he had always found attractive. But it was her courage since her stroke to struggle on, still writing and leading a life that was at least half way back to normal, that he found truly admirable.

Standing at the window and looking across the courtyard at the house opposite, he asked, 'Has this cottage been empty for long, Mrs Nevin—Beatrice?'

'It'll be about three months,' she answered. 'There was a young couple here over the winter, nice young people, quiet and no trouble, but they was looking for a house in Tolcaster where he'd a job and they found what they wanted about last Easter and moved out and I don't really know if Mr Cleaver advertised it after that or not. I remember he says to me once, he says, it's almost more bother than it's worth having tenants you know nothing about.

They can be noisy and they can park their cars so they gets
in your way and they can break things and the rent all goes
in taxes. So maybe he did nothing about it when Mr and
Mrs Stevens went. All I know is, he says to me one day,
"My brother's coming to stay in the cottage for the month
of August, Beatie, and it'll oblige us if you'll work for him
Tuesdays and Fridays, like you did for Mr and Mrs
Stevens." So of course I said I'd be glad to. I'd been coming in anyway all the time the cottage was empty, just to
make sure everything was all right, and giving it a bit of a
dust round in case it was suddenly wanted, but if you want
me I can come in two hours those two days, and if there's
any shopping you'd like me to do in the village you've only
to say, because I comes up to the house all the other days
and it'd be no trouble to bring over anything you want.'

'That's very good of you,' Gavin said. 'I'll be very grateful for your help.'

'No problem,' she went on. 'And if you look in the fridge
now, I think you'll find everything you want for your lunch.
There's a cold chicken and some potato salad and some
tomatoes and there's cheese and biscuits and all that. And
there's tea and coffee in the cupboard. Miss Astor brought
everything in yesterday. And there's drinks in here.'

She went to a corner cupboard and opened its door. Inside Gavin saw whisky and sherry and gin, some soda water
and some glasses. He was feeling just about ready for a
drink and was glad of it. But it crossed his mind to wonder
why he had not been invited to the other house for lunch.
He thought that it would have been a normal sort of thing
to do on his arrival. However, he had not actually told
Nigel when he would be arriving, as he had not known
how long the drive would take him, and all arrangements
seemed to have been made for his comfort in the cottage.

Mrs Nevin said that she would be off now, collected her
bicycle from where she had left it beside the front door,

mounted it and rode off. Gavin took his suitcase up the narrow staircase and unpacked it in the little bedroom in which the bed had been made up for him. It was covered with a patchwork bedspread, there were frilly chintz curtains at the small dormer window that had been pierced through the thatch of the roof, the ceiling was sloping and there was a built-in hanging cupboard and a rather battered mahogany chest of drawers with a mirror standing on it. The other bedroom, across the square yard of landing at the top of the stairs, was almost identical. The pale blue bathroom was miniature, but appeared to have everything requisite in it.

Gavin returned to the living-room, poured out some whisky for himself, went to the kitchen for water to add to it, glanced into the refrigerator and saw the chicken, the salad and the tomatoes there, then settled down in the one easy chair in the room and suddenly realized that he was glad not to have been invited to the other house for lunch. For what with the pressures of the end of term, the muddle and disappointment concerning the Hellenic cruise and the drive that morning, it was pleasant to be alone in quiet to relax.

He was not entirely pleased with himself because of this, wondering how much the fact that he had passed his fortieth birthday a fortnight ago might have to do with the feeling.

From where he sat he could see the house where Nigel and Annabel had lived for twelve years. Once upon a time, Gavin had heard, it had been a farmhouse, but the acres around it had long ago been sold off and now there was only a strip of garden which extended from one end of it, sloping slightly upwards, to where the downs began. There were two or three tall beech trees near the house, some rose-beds and flowering shrubs, and a stretch of well-kept lawn with a tall wooden fence at the end of it. Gavin knew that neither Nigel nor Annabel had ever been enthusiastic gardeners, so presumably they had found someone to look after it all for them.

The house was long and low, with casement windows and a roof of old red tiles on which moss was growing. Gavin had stayed in it a few times during the visits that he had occasionally paid to his brother and sister-in-law, but the visits had always been brief as he had generally been able to find more interesting things to do with his holidays, and though he had always thought the house inside very charming, he had never reached the stage of feeling at home in it.

How did Caroline like it, he suddenly wondered, Caroline the complete Londoner, the actress who had recently been achieving some success, Annabel's hitherto not very devoted half-sister? What on earth was she doing here?

He was able to ask Nigel this question about an hour later after having had two drinks, eaten some cold chicken, salad and cheese and seen a car drive up to the house opposite and Nigel go hurriedly into it. But he did not come to the cottage for about another half-hour. When he came he was full of apologies for not having been there to greet Gavin when he arrived.

'A committee meeting this morning,' he said, 'and I couldn't get away. I usually get home in good time for lunch and I wanted specially to be here today to see you, but I couldn't work it. I hope you've found everything in order.'

He was a tall man and, though he was ten years older than Gavin, still had a look of vitality about his slim, loose-limbed body, a look of almost explosive energy which, as Gavin remembered it, he had always had. There was a certain family resemblance between the brothers, though there was no question about it that Nigel was far the better-looking. His features were as fine but stronger, and there was none of the nervous diffidence about them that had brought the early wrinkles to Gavin's thin face. Nigel's hair was darker than Gavin's, with a slight wave in it and was beginning to be streaked with grey, which only helped to give him an air of distinction. He was casually dressed, but in a way that gave him an air of opulence.

This did not come from his work. He had a respectable job and one that Gavin believed he happened to enjoy, but which was not particularly highly paid. He was Director of the Cantlewell Museum in Tolcaster, a collection that had originally been formed, then donated to the town, by a Lord Cantlewell about the middle of the eighteenth century, then had been slowly added to, mostly by Cantlewell descendants, ever since that time. Nigel had begun life, after his stint as a pupil at Stillborough, like Gavin, by taking a Fine Arts degree and then a Ph.D. at the University of Edinburgh, had stayed on there for a time as a lecturer, then had moved south to become Deputy Director of the Cantlewell. For some years now he had been its Director, but before that had come about he had married Annabel Astor. Hence the well-cut casual suit that he was wearing and the fine old house at Upthorn. He liked fine things, though he had never troubled to have anything special in the way of a car. He was not in the least interested in anything mechanical and the car that stood in front of the house had probably been bought second-hand and at its best had not been notable.

Looking round the little living-room with the drink that Gavin had given him in his hand, he observed, 'Annabel did unload a lot of old junk here, didn't she? I hope at least it's comfortable. It's very good of you to come, Gavin. It'll do Annabel good. It isn't everyone who understands her these days, but with luck you will. She's really pretty lonely. And the worst of it is that if anyone's friendly to her she thinks they're pitying her and she bristles at it and says something offensive. Then of course they don't come again.'

'How is she?' Gavin asked. He had seen Annabel only once since her stroke when she had still been semi-paralysed and mentally confused. 'Mrs Nevin says she's still writing.'

'Yes, she manages to do that. Enjoys doing it. It does her good. She's made very good progress in the last few months.'

'Will it make much difference to you if she can't keep it up—financially, I mean?'

Nigel shrugged. 'Who knows? Not for some time, I should think. The paperbacks will keep rolling on for a while, even if she doesn't produce anything new. In any case, as things still are, after all her years of work, it isn't a thing we've got to worry about. But how about you, Gavin? Still stuck at Stillborough? You love that place. You did even when you were a kid there. I hated it, though I dare say no more than I'd have hated any other school I might have been sent to.'

Gavin did not think it was true that he exactly loved the school where he taught, but being there did give him a sense of security which had been lacking through most of his childhood. His mother had died when he was so young that he hardly remembered her and his father had been an engineer, working for one of the big oil companies, who had been continually on the move from one country to another, and had always kept his four children trailing along with him. When first Nigel and then much later Gavin had been old enough to be dumped in a public school in England, he had sent them off and from then on had had as little to do with them as possible. They had spent their holidays with a variety of aunts and uncles, sometimes welcome and made much of and sometimes obviously regarded as mere bur-densome obligations.

Their two sisters had had virtually no education at all,

their father regarding education, particularly for girls, as a lamentable expense and thinking that what he could hammer into their brains when he felt like it should be adequate for all their needs. So Stillborough, for Gavin, had been the nearest thing that he had ever known to a home, and being able to return there to teach, after his time at Oxford and a few years at a grammar school, had always seemed to him an incredible piece of good fortune.

'Have you seen anything of Barbara and Helena lately?' Nigel asked.

'Not for some time,' Gavin answered. 'I spent last Christmas with Helena, just for a few days, and except that she's getting quite an opinion of herself as a healer and seems to have an increasing number of visits from people who, as she puts it, have passed on, she seemed much the same as usual. But she drinks a good deal.'

Helena was the younger of his two sisters, only two years older than himself and in their childhood they had been fast friends. Her lively imagination had impressed him deeply and her frail prettiness had enchanted him. But though some of the prettiness was still there, she had never married or so far as he knew had a lover. She seemed to prefer her fantasies to flesh and blood relationships.

Yet there was a certain bitterness in her because no one had tried very hard to claim her. She felt that life had used her badly and that the few people, both men and women, who had tried to achieve some friendship with her, were incomprehensibly trying to hurt her. The discovery that some of them would accept her as a healer had done a great deal for her self-esteem and having friendships with the dead appeared to be very consoling.

Barbara, who was three years older than Helena, was very different. She was a tall, muscular woman with close-cropped grey hair and a deep, masculine voice. She was the widow of a man who had owned a small flower-farm in

Devon and she still lived on it, though she had leased most of the land to a neighbour, keeping only enough for herself to grow her own vegetables and maintain a few free-range chickens.

Her vegetables were grown on strictly organic lines. Not a trace of chemical fertilizer was ever allowed on her land. She was very fussy about her diet too, being ready to drive long distances to obtain meat and cheese and butter from other farmers who shared her beliefs, or at least persuaded her that they did. She never dreamt of buying anything at a supermarket. Yet her health, which was the main subject of her conversation, had never been outstandingly good. But her digestion would have been even worse than it was, so she asserted, if she had not been so careful about what she ate.

Her husband, luckily for him, had agreed with her in everything, but he had died relatively early and since his death a tendency that she had always had to be rude to anyone who disagreed with her in any way had markedly increased. Almost her only resemblance to Helena was that she was really a very lonely woman too and could not understand why this should be.

Neither sister had much money but this did not seem to concern them. All four Cleavers had small private incomes, inherited from a rich grand-aunt who had left her fortune divided among a collection of cousins, and though with inflation these incomes were becoming ever smaller, it had apparently never occurred to either of the sisters that their lives might be made more agreeable if they were to work for money. In fact, to have done so they would have thought rather contemptible. As long as they had roofs over their heads, enough to eat and to clothe themselves and to indulge their eccentricities, they did not worry about their economic situations.

Not that either of them thought of herself as eccentric.

The truly eccentric member of the family, they both thought, was Nigel. Nigel had married money. He had become rich. Furthermore, to achieve this, he had been driven to marrying a woman ten years older than himself, indeed a remarkable thing to do. Actually Annabel's money, Gavin believed, had had nothing to do with Nigel's marriage. He had married for love and for nothing else, love that appeared to have lasted for twenty years.

'I've always thought Helena would move in on you if you weren't careful,' Nigel said. 'You've always been her favourite.'

'If she hasn't managed it, it hasn't been for want of trying,' Gavin admitted. 'But it wouldn't really have been for love of me. I think she sees herself, with her strange gifts, as making an impression on the sort of small, close-knit community that we've got at Stillborough. She wouldn't, of course. She doesn't realize how deeply conventional we are and how we deplore any signs of oddity.'

'But that conventionality is just what appeals to you, isn't it?' Nigel said. 'Holding on to it makes you feel you've really got free at last from the influence of our dreadful old father.'

There was truth in this. Their father had been in many ways a strange man. He had been violent, not in actions that had led to any ill-treatment of his children, but in emotional moods in which he might shout at them in mysterious rages or literally shed tears of self-pity because no one appreciated him at his real value. He had drunk heavily and though Gavin had never seen him in a state that could really be called drunkenness, he had had a habit, when he was far enough through his bottle of whisky, of starting to read the Bible aloud. Yet he was not in the least a religious man. He read it, he claimed, for the sake of its sheer beauty and his reading, in a deep, rich voice, had been impressive. But one of the effects of this was that his children had grown up in a state of complete religious confusion, which Gavin believed was the reason why all of them, with perhaps the exception of Nigel, had sought beliefs of their own, whether in the importance of diet and organic farming, or in the healing power of the laying on of hands, which had given them some sense of stability.

Gavin's own belief, he was aware, was in merging into the throng of ordinary people and doing as little as possible to attract any attention to himself. The traditional quality of the public school system appealed to him deeply. To belong to it was to be accepted in the country where in reality he had no roots. Seeing this about himself, he could be ironic about it, could apparently laugh at himself for what Nigel called his conventionality, but that was merely a defence against criticism and not of much importance.

Nigel put down his empty glass and stood up.

'I must be getting back to work,' he said. 'But I was almost forgetting to say we hope you'll come over to dinner with us this evening. Our neighbours, the Jays, will be coming in. You'll like them. Desmond Jay's a doctor. He's a member of a practice in Tolcaster and their daughter Leslie works in an antique shop there. But our having arranged for them to come this evening was the main reason why you weren't asked over for lunch. Annabel said that if she'd got to make the effort of being sociable in the evening, she couldn't face the idea of having anyone, even you, in for lunch. I said I was sure that bread and cheese would do for you, but she stuck to it that having to talk to anyone twice in a day would be too much for her. And I don't argue with her when she gets something like that in her head. You'll have to forgive her for some peculiarities. You'll come, will you?'

'Of course—thank you,' Gavin said. 'But isn't Caroline there to run things for Annabel?'

'Yes, for the present,' Nigel answered. 'It's a godsend

having her. We've run through quite a series of house-keepers and it was sheer luck that when our last one departed, Caroline happened to be free. Wonderful girl. She's managing everything.'

'But how does she happen to be free?' Gavin asked. 'I thought she was more or less tied up for life in that television soap opera, *For Ever and a Day*. Did something go wrong with that?'

'According to her, her three-year contract came to an end and she chose not to renew it. She said she hated it from the beginning, not only because of the frightful stuff it is, but because of the atmosphere, the general back-stabbing and so on that went on behind the scenes, quite unlike the real theatre, she claims.'

Gavin had watched a few showings of *For Ever and a Day* when it had first appeared on the box, out of curiosity to see Caroline at work, but even for her sake he had not faced more of it than that, though he thought that whoever had originally devised it had had a rather profound idea. Most of the soap operas that had run for years in this country, so it seemed to him, were about working-class people, while those imported from America were of the very rich and powerful. But *For Ever and a Day* was strictly about the middle classes, and since what the majority of people now-adays, from the lowest to the highest, try to model themselves upon is the middle class, whether successful and even very wealthy, or poor but bearing that poverty with stoicism, good nature and good manners, the programme had been an immense success. The fantasies it supplied were not too hopelessly unattainable for anyone. Seeing Caroline playing her part in it, Gavin had assumed that she would soon be rich and famous.

Yet here she was in Upthorn, as housekeeper for her invalid sister, certainly not being paid for her services and without any outlet for her considerable talent.

'Well, I'm glad you've got her to help you,' he said. 'But I never suspected her of being domesticated.'

'She isn't, very,' Nigel said with a grin. 'Don't expect anything special of the dinner she lays on. But, dear girl, she does do her best. Come early, say about half past six, then you and she can have a get-together before the Jays arrive. You were good friends once, weren't you?'

'Yes,' Gavin said.

'In fact, I thought at one time . . . But I don't suppose you want to talk about that. As I said, it's very good of you to have come. I hope you're going to manage all right on your own here. You'll find our Beatie invaluable. Goodbye now for the present.'

Nigel let himself out of the cottage, crossed the courtyard to his decrepit car and drove away.

When he had gone Gavin thought of going for a walk. The smooth green slopes of the downs rising up just behind the stone house and the cottage looked empty, quiet and inviting, and the afternoon was fine with a light breeze blowing and a sky of clear blue with only a few puffs of white cloud travelling slowly across it. But there was something else that he wanted to do. He wanted to see Caroline.

He had been looking forward to it all day, though with a trace of fear in his anticipation, for he did not know what effect she would have on him now. In the past, when they might have drifted into marriage if her career and her ambition had not led her to evade any close personal commitment, he had been through a painful time, even if he had not been quite heart-broken. But it seemed that she had now abandoned the career and besides that was five years older. What differences might those years have made in her? And until he had met her, how could he tell what differences they might truly have made in himself?

His impatience to see her had grown in him ever since he had arrived here. Only a day or two ago he would have been ready to state sincerely that seeing her was a matter of only moderate importance to him, yet now it seemed something that ought to be done as soon as possible. Perhaps that was merely because he wanted to get it over so that he could feel at peace again, something to be taken quickly and swallowed down as rapidly as possible, a dose of what might be disagreeable medicine. Not that he could imagine it being actually disagreeable. It might be a shock. It might revive the old pain. On the other hand, it might set him free.

After changing his mind about it several times, he suddenly left the cottage, strode resolutely across the courtyard and hammered with the iron knocker on the heavy old oak door of the house opposite.

CHAPTER 2

No one came to answer his knocking. When the sound had died there was only silence, as there had been in the morning. He knocked again. When there was still no answer it occurred to him that Caroline might be one of the people who liked to lie down in the afternoons and that she might be upstairs in her bedroom, sound asleep. A sense of half-angry disappointment filled him. At her age she ought not to be lying down at this time of day. Surely Upthorn was not a place where the habit of the siesta was cultivated.

However, it seemed that it was no use waiting. He turned away, but he had taken only a couple of steps when the door behind him was opened and Caroline stood there. She had a sleepy look as if indeed she had only just been wakened, but she was as disturbingly lovely as ever, tall, slim, dark-haired, with great dark eyes in a smoothly tanned face and a wide, expressive mouth. As he turned towards her she put both arms round his neck and kissed him on both cheeks, murmuring in her soft voice, 'Darling, it's just heaven to see you again. I've hardly been able to wait for this.'

He knew at once that he did not believe her.

For one thing, if she had really been so impatient to see him, all she would have had to do was to come to the cottage an hour or so earlier. Calling him darling, of course, in her profession meant nothing. But also the kiss on both cheeks somehow meant very little. He always felt when he was encountered by this popular greeting that it was really more formal than a kiss on one cheek would have been. He felt as if he had been promptly put in his place, in the kindest way, of course, but still informed that he was to expect nothing from her.

She had changed, he thought, since he had seen her last. She had grown, if anything, more beautiful, with an air of calm and depth that she had not had before. Behind the superficial demonstrativeness was something that was new to her. She must be nearly forty, he reckoned, almost the same age as himself. Her father had married young and the child of that marriage had been Annabel, but it had ended fairly soon in divorce and it had been many years before he had nerved himself to try again. When he did so it had startled everyone that he had been capable of producing a child, but that child had been Caroline who had been left orphaned while she was still an infant and who had been brought up mostly by an aunt and by her half-sister. Their relationship seemed never to have been a really warm one, but perhaps, Gavin thought, it was gratitude for the care that she had received in those early days that had brought Caroline to Upthorn now that Annabel needed her.

She was in a pale yellow sleeveless cotton dress, was bare-legged and had on a pair of floppy-looking white sandals. Her arms and her legs were tanned as smoothly as her face, on which she wore no make-up. Her hair was drawn straight back from her face and tied with a strip of black ribbon. She looked cool and fresh and tempting. Gavin would have liked to take her in his arms at once and give her a very much more convincing embrace than she had given him.

Instead he said, 'Am I interrupting anything? Shall I come another time?'

'No, didn't I say I'm glad to see you?' She put a hand on his sleeve and drew him indoors. 'Let's go and sit in the garden and you can tell me everything that's been happening to you. Annabel's lying down. She always does in the afternoons. We shan't disturb her.'

Gavin stepped into the hall, which was stone-paved with a curving staircase, carpeted in dark red, rising opposite the door to the floor above. A door on the right led into the drawing-room and another on the left into the dining-room, from which, as he knew, a door led straight into the kitchen. There were one or two other doors into other rooms, one of which was called Nigel's study. The ceiling of the hall, like the walls, was white with one dark beam across it. A table to the side of the staircase had a telephone and a bowl of Burmese silver on it, filled with bright zinnias. It was unpretentious, yet impressive. So was the drawing-room through which Caroline led him, though here the walls were papered in narrow gold and white stripes. There was an old carpet which he knew was a fairly valuable Savonnerie covering most of the stone floor and the furniture was unexpectedly modern, which probably added to the comfort of the room, if it gave it a touch of strangeness. An old fireplace with a crooked beam across the top of it had an unlit fire of logs laid in the open grate. Glass doors, a fairly recent innovation in the room, opened at one end of it on to a narrow terrace on which there were some comfortable

wicker chairs. Caroline dropped into one of them and gestured to Gavin to sit in one beside it.

'Tea?' she said. 'I'll get some presently, but first tell me
just how you are and how life's been treating you and why
you've come here. Why *have* you come here, Gavin?'

'Because Nigel suggested it when I'd no other plans,' he
answered. 'I was going on a cruise with a friend, but that
fell through. But why have you come here, Caroline? That
seems to me a much more interesting question.'

'I seemed to be needed,' she said. 'Anyway, someone was
needed and I happened to be free.'

'But how did you happen to be free? I thought you were
tied up for ever with that soap-opera in which you seemed
to be doing so well.'

She smiled. 'My contract came to an end so I thought
I'd get out while the going was good. Really it was awful,
working in the thing, Gavin. I was miserable.'

'Are you particularly enjoying life here?'

'D'you think that's all one ever ought to do—enjoy life?'

'Why not?'

'You don't really. You only think it's all I've ever cared
about. I'm a little older than when we last saw each other,
my dear, and I've a bit of a conscience now that's just capable of giving me an occasional jolt.'

'So that's really and truly why you came, is it? Did Nigel
suggest it, or was it your own idea?'

'A bit of each. I came down on what was meant to be a
short visit and I saw what a mess they were getting into
with their latest housekeeper just about to leave and Annabel really rather frightened about it and Nigel getting desperate. She never could understand why she couldn't keep
anyone. She was sure she was perfectly sweet to them all
and so she was after her fashion, but I admit she can get
on my nerves at times and I've been used to her all my life.
She's so determined you've got to admire her and keep on

showing it. She demands all sorts of little attentions which can make you feel a bit menial and that simply won't do nowadays, even if she thanks you for them over and over again. Anyway, I think it was I who suggested I might stay on for a time, and that's somehow lasted.'

'And you're contented?'

'Reasonably.' She gave him another smile, but there was a touch of sadness in this one which made a remarkable change in her expressive face. 'You don't honestly believe I'm capable of a disinterested action, do you?'

'I admit it puzzles me,' he said. 'You've a talent which you seem to be wasting. And it's always appeared to me that a person who has any real talent is driven by that more strongly than by anything else, even if they don't entirely want to be. Look at Annabel. As I understand it, she's a very sick woman, yet she can't stop writing. And that can't be because she and Nigel need money, because they've more than enough to last them for the rest of their lives.'

He did not understand the look she gave him. There was a kind of pitying mockery in it.

'So you'd call what she's got a talent,' she said.

'Of its kind. Putting it at its lowest, it's a talent for making money. But the truth about it is, whatever the quality of the product, it must be so important to her that it's helping to keep her going.'

'Oh yes, it's important to her.'

He was puzzled at her tone. 'You almost sound as if you think it isn't, but for her to keep going now must take a pretty tremendous effort.'

'Of course the only question is, what is it about it that's so important?' she said. 'But now suppose we talk about you. You're contented, are you? You don't think you might be wasting some great talent?'

'I've never thought I had one,' he answered. 'And yes,

I'm as contented as most people ever are. Perhaps even more so.'

'You don't look a day older than when I saw you last.'

That was the kind of thing that she was given to saying that had always irritated him. She hardly troubled to make it sound as if she meant it, yet she seemed to think it necessary to say things of that nature, as if they were part of the business of being a charming woman. For a few minutes, while they had been talking, she had sounded thoughtful and sincere, but that had suddenly gone.

'I'd have expected you to be bored as hell at that frightful school,' she said. 'You should hear what Nigel has to say about it.'

'It happens that I like teaching,' Gavin said. 'I even like the young male, particularly on those rather rare occasions when he wants to learn something. A little of that can make up for a fair amount of that boredom you talk about.' He did not try to tell her how much the sense of belonging in a securely settled community meant to him. Perhaps if he had really had some positive talent he might have been prepared to stand alone, but that was something that he had never believed about himself.

'All the same, darling, I'm sure you're wasting yourself,' she said. 'I'm sure you could have been a lawyer or a doctor and made a great name for yourself and even got a knighthood. You were always the clever one of the family, though don't tell Nigel I said so. He's really so vain, isn't he? But I've always adored him. He's angelic to Annabel.' She was still using the light, unconvincing tone which made Gavin feel that undoubtedly she thought him a fool. 'Now you'd like some tea, wouldn't you? I won't be a minute.'

She stood up and went quickly back into the house through the open door of the drawing-room.

Gavin stayed where he was, gazing across the garden

towards the downs. He saw a pigeon strut across the lawn, stay for a little, then fly heavily off. The sky was still the same clear blue and the leaves of the beeches stirred only faintly in the light breeze. There was silence except for the song of a bird, but he did not know enough about birds to identify it. He thought how pleasant it must be to live in a place like this if you had a reason for being there. Stillborough was a small town, once attractive but being rapidly spoilt by the developers. The centre of it was ancient and there were a few dignified Georgian terraces, but on the one side it degenerated into unimpressive middle-class surburbia and on the other into slums. There were several factories now on the outskirts of the town which had not been built yet when Gavin went to live there.

The school was about a mile from the edge of the town, with fair-sized playing-fields and grounds around it, but bungalows had been creeping up the road towards it and were threatening to encircle it. Gavin lived in a two-room flat on the upper floor of a house that belonged to the games master, just outside the gates at the end of the drive that led up to the school buildings. The house had been built in the 'twenties, was sufficiently comfortable but had not much character, and as he had never been much interested in his surroundings provided that he had plenty of room for his books, for a few pictures, one really good chair and a desk at which he could sit and type in comfort, he had never troubled to make much of it. His landlord was a brawny young man with a wife and two young children, all of them good-natured though unfortunately addicted to turning up the sound of their television rather too loudly and for a time this had troubled Gavin and he had thought of complaining, but he always shrank from complaining unless he was really driven to it and by now he was so used to the noise that he hardly heard it and he actually enjoyed the wild cries of the children, a girl and a boy, when they took to brawling in the garden. On the whole he thought himself reasonably well off.

But certainly the place had not the charm of this quiet old house and garden at Upthorn. All the same, now that he was here, what was he going to do with himself for the next few weeks? So far he had hardly considered that. He was not easily bored but it would be advisable for him, he thought, to find something to do. He could not spend all his time visiting Caroline and his brother and sister-in-law.

He had just reached the point of deciding that he would ask if they had such a thing as a local guide-book so that he could begin by exploring the sights of the neighbourhood when his thoughts were interrupted by a sound of tapping behind him and then of dragging footsteps. He got hurriedly to his feet to greet Annabel.

The tapping came from the thin black cane on which she supported herself. She moved very slowly. She smiled and held out a hand to him. The simple linen dress that she was wearing, which fitted a little too snugly over her heavy body so that if anything it increased her look of weight, was a bright blue, a colour of which she had always been very fond because she believed that it matched her eyes. Her pale gold hair was cleverly arranged and her oval face, which Gavin thought had sagged a good deal more than when he had seen her last, was carefully made-up. She wore pearls which he knew were genuine and a big ring of sapphires on one finger.

'Where's Caroline gone to?' she asked as she lowered herself cautiously into a chair.

'She said she was going to get some tea,' Gavin answered.

'Ah, that's good,' she said. 'I feel like a cup of tea. And how are you, Gavin, my dear? It seems years since we last saw you.'

'It is a fair time. I'm much as usual. But how are you?'

'Much as usual too.' She gave a hoarse little laugh. 'That isn't saying much. I'm a wreck, as you can see. But I do my best to keep going. Actually, I'm a good deal better than I was. For a time I could hardly walk at all and my poor old brain was in a state of total confusion. When anyone spoke to me it seemed to take a minute or two for what they said to reach me. So they thought I was deaf and used to repeat what they'd said, shouting at me. You don't know how humiliating that was. Sometimes I used to feel as if I'd like to kill them all, really I did. I don't suppose that surprises you. You're one of the people who've always known I was more than a bit of a bitch.'

Gavin thought that more people had always known this than she had realized.

'But you're writing again,' he said, 'so that's cleared up, even if getting about is still a bit difficult.'

'Oh, they've told you that, have they?'

'Yes.'

'But what did they say about what I'd written?'

He thought about it. 'I don't think anything in particular. They were just admiring you for the way you've fought your way back to doing it. As I do too.'

She gave her brief laugh again. 'But you've said to yourself, "Another couple of the usual old Annabel Astors." Oh, I know what you think of me. Now tell the truth, have I ever given you the impression that I expected you to like my books?'

'No, Annabel, you haven't. You've always been very tolerant.'

'Only I'd like to know what other people have said about them. They've really said nothing—Nigel or Caroline?'

'I don't think so, no.'

'I'd just like to know if they think they're the same as usual, not a lot worse, or even—it isn't impossible—rather better. You see, I've had a lot of time to think.'

She was looking at him with a strange, questioning intensity in her brilliant eyes, as if she were watching him in case he betrayed some falsity that she suspected.

He shook his head. 'We didn't actually get around to discussing that.'

It would be difficult for her to realize, he thought, that they would have had anything to talk of but herself.

She leant her head back in her chair, looking suddenly very old and dejected.

'My own view of the things is that they're lousy, but the publishers don't seem to mind, as long as they've got my name on them. I don't know how much longer I can go on getting away with it, I mean if they're really getting worse. Now tell me, what really brought you here this summer? You've never been all that anxious to come before.'

'I think I must have been attracted by the thought of a little peace and quiet.'

'Peace and quiet plus a little Caroline.'

He did not answer.

After a moment, with one of her sardonic smiles, she said, 'Isn't that the truth? Are you still in love with her, Gavin?'

'I suppose I might say that's something I rather want to find out.'

'You'll never get anywhere with her, you know.'

'Perhaps not.'

'Why don't you ask, "Is there anyone else?"'

'Well, is there?'

'Not a soul, to the best of my knowledge, but it would have been normal for you to ask, wouldn't it?'

'Well, if there isn't anyone, why haven't I a chance, if I should happen to want one?'

'Because the dear girl is simply incapable of loving anyone. She hasn't got a heart. I'd have expected you to have discovered that by now. You've always been rather quick at understanding other people.'

He discovered that he could be cruel. 'Would you say it was heartless to give up her career to come and look after you?'

'Good gracious, that isn't why she came! Whatever gave you that idea?'

'It seems a rather obvious one to deduce from the circumstances.'

She put out the hand with the great ring on it and patted him on the sleeve.

'If that's what you like to think, don't let me trouble you. I'd hate to trouble you. I've always been very fond of you, Gavin. Have you realized that? I think you're really the nicest member of the family, much nicer than Nigel, you know, though you were of course rather young for me to have been able to marry you. I'm sorry about Caroline. And here she comes with the tea. Just in time to stop me saying something really awful.'

Caroline reappeared on the terrace, pushing a tea-trolley. Gavin had a cup of tea and a chocolate biscuit, but did not stay much longer. Something about his encounters with the two sisters dismayed him, though he was not sure what it was. It might be, he thought, Annabel's certainty that he had been in love with Caroline, together with her obvious belief that that was still the case with him. He did not like to be taken so for granted when he himself was not sure of his condition. It tended to drive him back into himself, making him resentful of this intrusion into his feelings.

Besides that there was something that grated on him about the relationship between the two women. He wondered how much they had ever really cared for one another. But if Caroline was not strongly attached to the sister who had been almost a mother to her, what was she doing here?

And if Annabel was not at least grateful for what Caroline was doing for her now, why did she speak of her in that slighting way? Was that merely the jealousy that the old and sick can feel for the young and vigorous? In another mood might she be loving and appreciative?

Whatever the truth was, Gavin began to feel rather glad as he went back to the cottage that when he returned to the house in the evening the Jay family would be present to mask those persisting family tensions which he recognized had always been there. He had first met Caroline in Nigel's and Annabel's house one Christmas, and because there had always been so little affection in his own family, it had not occurred to him to wonder at an apparent lack of it between the sisters. Yet he had been aware of it even then. And remembering that he returned to puzzling over what Caroline was doing here now, attending dutifully to Annabel's needs.

A sense of duty, he would have thought, was not one of Caroline's more marked characteristics. But perhaps he was wrong there. Perhaps, all but concealed behind the quick changes in her from superficial warmth and demonstrativeness to a rather enigmatic kind of thoughtfulness, there was a capacity for gratitude and love. He had often considered the matter and was inclined to believe that that was the truth.

It was half past six when he went back to the house. Nigel had returned by then and was in the drawing-room with Annabel, both with drinks in their hands. Caroline, Gavin presumed, was in the kitchen, attending to the dinner. The Jays had not arrived yet, but they came soon afterwards, Dr Desmond Jay, his wife Marion and their daughter Leslie. Nigel kissed Marion and Leslie on both cheeks and Desmond Jay kissed Annabel on both of hers. She was sitting on a sofa of black plastic and steel and had not attempted to rise when the Jays came in through the open door into the garden, but she had her stick within reach and used it now to beckon Marion Jay to come and sit beside her.

She was a plump, pretty woman in her fifties with a cloud of curly grey hair and friendly grey eyes. She was wearing a grey and white striped silk dress and a pair of small coral earrings.

Sitting down beside Annabel, she exclaimed, 'Annabel, you're looking so *well*! I do think you're wonderful.' She looked up at Gavin. 'Don't you think she's wonderful, Mr Cleaver?—No, I'm going to call you Gavin. I've heard so much about you, I feel I know you. Annabel, I've just finished reading your latest *Love Late and Soon*. Of course I'll read it again. D'you know, I honestly don't know how often I've read most of your books, because each time I do they seem to me as fresh and exciting and surprising as the last time I read them. Truly, you're wonderful.'

'You can only go on re-reading things like that, if you really do, because they've made so little impression on you that you simply don't remember them,' Annabel said rather drily.

'What d'you mean, if I really do?' Marion Jay cried. 'Would I say I had if I hadn't? Is that what you think of me?'

'Well, perhaps you wouldn't,' Annabel said. 'But some people would. I don't trust compliments.'

Desmond Jay said, 'It's true you're looking better, Annabel.' He turned to Gavin. 'She's made a splendid recovery and my view of that is that it's been done by sheer will-power. Guts and determination. And that's particularly lucky for my wife because I don't know what she'd do if she didn't know there was another Annabel Astor coming out soon. When's the next one due, Annabel?'

He looked about the same age as his wife and was a tall, heavily built man, dark-haired but beginning to go bald, with thick, straight eyebrows above big, observant dark eyes. His face was square and brown with the beginnings of a double chin under a strong jaw.

'I believe in October,' Annabel answered. 'Or perhaps November or December. I can never keep count.'

'I'm sure you know to the day when the next book will be published,' Leslie Jay said in a mildly satirical tone. 'What's the title?'

She was small and slim and might have been anything between twenty-five and thirty and probably she would not look much older when she was forty. She had the smooth, creamy kind of skin that does not wrinkle, grey eyes like her mother's and soft brown hair brushed forward in a wavy fringe over her forehead. It was the colour that her mother's had probably been before it turned grey. There was a good deal of resemblance between them, except for the plumpness of the one and the slenderness of the other. Leslie was wearing close-fitting black trousers, a black and white patterned blouse and long gold tassels of earrings. She had no make-up on except for some vivid pink lipstick and some shiny pink nail-varnish on her small, thin hands. Gavin would probably have found her attractive if at the time his imagination had not been filled with the image of Caroline.

While Annabel was assuring Leslie that she never told anyone her titles in advance of publication, he was wondering what Caroline could be cooking that was keeping her so long in the kitchen. When presently she appeared and after having a quick drink summoned them all to the dining-room, it turned out to be smoked salmon, followed by a casserole of veal and mushrooms which might have been very good if the sauce had not somehow got clotted into lumps and some carrots that nestled amongst these had not been curiously hard, as if Caroline had forgotten to include them in the dish in the first place, then had belatedly added them. Gavin remembered Nigel's comment that when it came to cooking she at least did her best. However, the Côtes du Rhône was good if not outstanding, and the dining-room, with its white walls, long, mahogany table, Sheraton chairs, an old bureau in one corner, scarlet velvet curtains and a blue and white Copenhagen dinner service, was pleasing.

He found himself seated between Marion Jay and Leslie. Annabel was at one end of the table and Nigel at the other. Desmond Jay did most of the talking and most of what he talked about was cricket. He was secretary of the local cricket club and next day, if some medical emergency did not upset his plans, would be playing in a match against the village of Nether Thorn. He laughed at himself for his own enthusiasm and made no claim to any competence in the game, yet plainly he felt that it was one of the major contributions that England had made to civilization, even if in these days they hardly ever won any matches. He was proud of his association with it.

Nigel, toying with a piece of veal in coagulated sauce, gave a laugh.

'One of the best days of my life,' he said, 'was when it suddenly dawned on me, when I was about fourteen, that when I grew up I should never have to play a single game of cricket again. Adults, I realized, only did that if they really wanted to and I knew I wasn't going to want to. I was at that awful school, Stillborough, where Gavin's so happy, and that moment of understanding of how wonderful it would be to be grown up is still so vivid to me that I could describe to you the exact spot where I was standing when this illumination happened. It was in the drive just outside what we called the boot hole, where we changed our shoes when we had to go out and play some beastly game. If I were an artist I could paint it for you, boots and all in the background.'

'And you?' Leslie said, turning to Gavin. 'Are you as prejudiced as your brother?'

She had a low, pleasant voice, but there was a glint in her eyes that he did not understand. He wondered if the truth was that she disliked Nigel.

'On the whole I think games are very nice for other people,' he answered. 'I'm sure they're good for adolescent boys who've got a lot of steam to work off, though there are a few notable exceptions like Nigel. They never did him any good. My own ambition when I had to play anything was to be just good enough at it to be inconspicuous.'

'But that's how Gavin approaches everything,' Caroline said. 'He's so determined to be inconspicuous at all costs that it sometimes makes him quite noticeable.'

'Jerome, my first husband, was wonderful at cricket and golf and tennis and swimming, but what a bastard he was,' Annabel observed, suddenly entering the conversation after having seemed to be quite withdrawn from it, and though she spoke now she looked as if she were concentrating in- tently on something on her plate and not on the other people at the table. It made Gavin wonder all at once if she had some difficulty in managing her food, if her hands, perhaps as an after-effect of her illness, were very slightly paralysed. He remembered that he had noticed the same thing about her when he was having tea with her and Caro- line on the terrace, though he had not paid any attention to it then. She was a brave woman, he thought, to make herself live as nearly normally as she did.

But it surprised him to hear her speak of Jerome Halli- day. She very seldom did. She had married him when she was nineteen and the marriage, so Gavin had heard, had not lasted long. He had no doubt that between the time when it had ended and the time when she had first met Nigel, when she was nearly forty, there had been other men in her life, but this was merely something that Gavin had deduced from the fact that she had been both a beautiful and passionate woman, not from any confidence of hers. She spoke very little about her past life, apart from her experiences with publishers and agents and audiences to whom she had lectured about her work. She would talk about these for as long as her hearers would allow her to do so.

A silence followed what she had said, as if everyone there was as surprised as Gavin at hearing her speak of Jerome Halliday. She appeared to realize this, for she gave her throaty laugh.

'Poor old Jerome, he must be nearly seventy by now,' she said, 'if he's still alive.'

'Don't you know?' Leslie asked.

'My dear, I haven't heard anything about him for years,' Annabel said. 'I wonder what he does now instead of his cricket and all. I suppose he can still drive fast cars. He'd like that. I don't think he'd care much for bridge. Too slow for him. Of course, he may have kept up his golf. That's a good game for the elderly. When are you going to start taking golf seriously, Desmond?'

'When I've retired and have some time on my hands,' he answered.

'And that's a long way off,' his wife said. 'Of course he pretends sometimes he's looking forward to it, but really I think he'll feel as lost without his work as you would without your own, Annabel. You're an example to us all.'

'But apparently not to Caroline,' Leslie murmured to Gavin, speaking almost in a whisper so that what she said perhaps was not heard on the other side of the table. 'She seems to have been only too glad to retire at an early age. I might give it some thought myself sometime. Why should I drive off into Tolcaster every morning, day in day out, when I'm only paid a pittance and haven't a hope of ever doing anything important? But we all have this fixation nowadays that one ought to have a job.'

'I believe you work in an antique shop, don't you?' Gavin said.

She nodded.

'Isn't that interesting?' he asked.

'I can think of a dozen things I'd sooner do,' she said.

'For instance?'

'Marry and have a home and two children.' She gave a laugh, but went on, 'Oh, I'm quite serious about that. And I don't even insist there's got to be a lot of money to go with it. Just not that awful getting up every morning and getting in the car and driving off and being nice to the very few customers who wander into the shop.' In spite of her smile, there was an undertone of bitterness in her voice which made Gavin wonder if a man whom she would have liked to marry did not think of the matter quite as she did. 'You aren't married, are you?'

'No.'

'And never have been?'

'No.'

'Haven't you ever wanted to be?'

'Oh, often.'

'That probably means you haven't.'

Annabel broke in once more. 'Jerome's second wife wasn't in the least athletic, but I believe she adored it in him. Or so I heard. I never met her myself. We'd drifted apart before he ever encountered her. Poor Jerome, he must have found it a nuisance that she was a Catholic and very moral. It was marriage or nothing on that occasion, but he must have been really infatuated. I've sometimes wondered how it worked out.'

'Yet you don't even know if they're alive or dead,' Marion said.

'I haven't the slightest idea,' Annabel replied. 'You

know, I've only two souvenirs of my days with Jerome. One's this ring I'm wearing. It was my engagement ring and he actually thought I ought to give it back to him when we separated, but I wasn't having that. It's a very pretty ring, I think. We chose it together, and I like it. I often wear it.'

'Oh, I've often admired it,' Marion said. 'But I doubt if I could bring myself to wear it if I was in your place. Don't you feel there's a rather terrible sort of sadness about it? It must have meant so much to you once.'

Something that seemed odd to Gavin happened at that moment. He saw Desmond Jay look at Caroline, and there was the undisguised glitter of desire in his eyes. And Caroline, Gavin thought, was aware of it and mildly amused.

'Well, all it is to me now is a very pretty ring,' Annabel replied to Marion.

'And what was the second souvenir you've got?' Leslie asked.

Annabel looked around the table and slowly a smile appeared on her face.

'I'll show it to you,' she said. 'You'll be fascinated.'

Gripping the edge of the table in front of her, she started to get up.

Caroline said sharply, 'Annabel, don't!'

Nigel was looking disturbed. He also started to stand up, then seemed to change his mind and sank down once more on to his chair.

'Annabel, please!' he said.

But Annabel had levered herself to her feet and taken hold of the stick that was hooked over the back of her chair.

'It won't take a minute. It'll amuse you.' Still smiling, she started to make her way towards the old mahogany bureau in a corner of the room. 'You know, I haven't looked at the thing for ages. Of course, I oughtn't to have kept it. I don't really know why I did except for that feeling

one has about things that they may come in useful sometime.'

She had reached the bureau and pulled open the bottom
drawer. First moving one or two things in it, she reached
down and drew out something wrapped carefully in a yellow duster. Leaning her stick against the bureau so that she
had both hands free, she unwrapped the object, letting the
duster drop to the ground. She turned then, pointing a re-
volver at them all.

She started to laugh.

'If you could see your faces! You don't suppose it's
loaded, do you? Jerome brought it back from Germany
after the war, just to remind him of those dear old days
when he'd had a chance to kill people. But he forgot it when
he moved out and I've had it ever since. I'd hate to part
with it.'

'Annabel, please,' Nigel said in a soothing, very reasonable tone, 'don't ever point a gun at anyone, even if it isn't
loaded. Don't do it.'

She went on laughing, but the laughter was beginning to
sound a little hysterical.

'Are you afraid it really may be loaded?' she cried. The
hand holding the gun began to wobble, so that it pointed
from one person to another at the table. 'You think I'm a
bit crazy, don't you? That's what you've thought about me
ever since my stroke. You needn't pretend, you know. I can
see through you. You're all so bloody sympathetic, but you
think I'm mad.'

She took a step towards the table, laughing more and
more wildly. Her foot caught in the edge of the carpet that
covered most of the floor and she fell with a heavy crash to
the ground.

The gun went off and the bullet smashed through the
glass of the window.

CHAPTER 3

Nigel and Desmond Jay were at Annabel's side in a moment. She had fallen on her face. The gun lay beside her. Moaning a little, she stirred and tried to sit up.

'Sorry—so sorry—so stupid of me,' she said thickly.

'Take it easy,' Jay said. 'Don't try to hurry. Take your time.'

'I'm all right,' she muttered. 'Perfectly all right. I've done it before, you know—caught my foot at the edge of a rug and fallen down—no one there to help me then, but I got to my feet all right. Shouldn't have rugs to trip over in the house at all with someone like me around, so I've been told. But I'm quite all right. Don't worry.'

With the aid of Nigel and the doctor she staggered to her feet. They guided her to a chair and helped her to settle down in it.

'How scared you all look,' she said and managed a little giggle. 'Really it's nothing. Just leaves me feeling a bit shaken, but it'll soon pass off.'

She appeared to have forgotten all about the gun.

Gavin looked at it suspiciously as it lay innocently on the carpet.

'Do you suppose there are any more bullets in this thing?' he asked.

'Bullets—more bullets?' Marion Jay cried. 'Oh, goodness me! We ought to make sure there aren't. But probably there are. Oh, what a horrible thought!'

'Annabel, do you know?' Caroline stooped over the gun to look at it closely, but did not touch it.

Annabel was pale and was breathing deeply as if the

exertions of the last few moments had been too much for her.

'As a matter of fact—haven't the faintest idea—never thought of it being loaded,' she brought out in gasps. 'Funny thing, isn't it, to have a gun in the house for years and never even thought of it being loaded?'

'It might not have been a funny thing at all,' Nigel said. 'We had a lucky escape. But we ought to find out if there are any more bullets in the thing. Do any of you know anything about guns? I've never even handled one.'

Gavin shook his head. 'Neither have I.'

'And I can't say I have either,' Desmond Jay said. 'I recommend treating it with extreme caution.'

'We'll have to get hold of someone to mend the window, won't we?' Annabel said. She was beginning to sound quite cheerful. 'Such a nuisance. And being the weekend we'll never be able to get hold of anybody.'

'D'you mean there are three strong men in this room, and not one of them dares even to pick up the thing?' Leslie said. 'Perhaps you need a woman's touch.' She stooped quickly and was just about to pick up the gun when her father caught her arm and pulled her back.

'Now don't be a fool,' he said. 'We want to give this some careful consideration.'

'I think I'll put it back in the drawer for the present,' Nigel said. 'We can't just leave it lying there.'

Bending down, he very carefully picked up the gun, wrapped it once more in the yellow duster which had fallen to the floor and placed it in the drawer from which Annabel had taken it.

As he closed it Annabel said, 'Now we can have Caroline's apricot mousse. I know she made an apricot mousse this morning and she's good at mousses. It's one of the things she can do. I'm so sorry I interrupted everything in that stupid way.'

'Of course, if you want someone who knows about guns,' Marion said, 'there's Oliver.'

'Yes, of course,' Nigel agreed. 'Oliver.'

'That's right,' Desmond Jay said, 'Oliver.'

Gavin was about to ask who Oliver was when Annabel chuckled and said, 'But honestly, if you could have seen your faces!'

It was at that point that Gavin began to ask himself if Annabel's mind had been affected by her illness more than he had been told, and that when she had accused them all of thinking that she was mad she had not been far wrong.

For the rest of the evening, however, she appeared perfectly normal and they ate Caroline's apricot mousse and they had coffee and brandy in the drawing-room. He offered to help Caroline with the washing-up, but she told him that everything would go into the dishwasher and she would leave the stacking of it until later. The Jays left at half past ten and Gavin followed them out. As he left the house he found them still standing in the courtyard, as if they had been waiting for him; as it turned out that they had. Marion Jay said that she hoped he would come to have drinks with them during the weekend and he said that he would look forward to it.

But they still hesitated about going home, then Desmond Jay said, 'I'm wondering what you made of that episode, Cleaver. Do you think Annabel honestly didn't know the gun was loaded, or was she having a bit of fun, giving us all a fright?'

Gavin had not thought about that. 'I took it for granted she didn't know,' he said.

'It's just that Nigel and Caroline seemed very worried when they realized why she was making for the bureau,' Jay said.

'You mean you think they knew what was there and that

they knew it was loaded,' Gavin said. 'I can't see that some-how. If they'd known, wouldn't they have stopped her even taking it out of the drawer? My impression was that they were simply worried because of the rather strange mood she was in. Is she often like that, do you know?'

'You've known her much longer than we have,' Jay said. 'We've only lived here three years and we haven't seen much of her till recently.'

'I've never seen much of her,' Gavin said. They were wandering slowly round the courtyard and as they approached the door of the cottage he wondered if he ought to ask them in for one more drink. 'But she must be basically all right if she's still writing.'

'But is she?' Desmond Jay said.

Gavin looked at him in surprise. 'Well, isn't she? I've been told she is.'

'Oh, probably you're right.' Jay's thick, straight eye-brows were drawn together in a worried frown. 'It's just that I've thought that possibly she had them in store. Someone as prolific as she's always been might easily have one or two put by to bring out when, say, she felt like a holiday, yet wanted to keep the supply going. And now, when really she's ill, she wants people to go on thinking she's capable of producing them still. She hates being treated as if she's ill, but of course she is.'

'May I ask who Oliver is?' Gavin asked. 'The one who knows about guns.'

Leslie gave a laugh. 'Yes, he does know about guns. He's Dr Penbury, a partner of my father's. And he belongs to some sort of gun club. I don't know much about it, except that he's won one or two prizes and for sure could tell us if that was a Smith and Wesson or a Luger, or whatever.'

'Anyway, I'm very sorry for Annabel,' Marion said in her quiet kindly way, 'whether she's quite responsible for her actions or not. I think it's so wonderful of Caroline to have stayed on to look after her. I don't know what they'd do without her.'

'Yes, Caroline's quite a girl,' Desmond Jay assented. There was something in his tone that troubled Gavin. It seemed to mean a little too much.

'Even if she can't cook anything but mousses,' Leslie said.

As they were now opposite his door he invited them in, but they refused and with Marion repeating that they hoped to see him again during the weekend and would telephone, they went on towards the gate. Gavin unlocked his door and let himself into the small sitting-room of the cottage.

Automatically he relocked the door on the inside and bolted it, then suddenly wondered if that was normal practice here in the country, as it was in Stillborough. But then he thought that nowadays it was often in the most isolated places that the most horrifying crimes take place. Solitary old women of eighty get raped and strangled. Children get kidnapped and their bodies are found in ditches, battered to death. Petrol is poured through letter-boxes and set on fire for apparently no reason. But why were such things on his mind tonight? Was it the absurd incident of Annabel and the gun?

He went upstairs to bed and slept soundly.

Next morning he woke soon after seven, made up his mind to get up, though if he had been at home he would probably have stayed in bed for another hour, went downstairs in his dressing-gown and made coffee and toast. Putting it on a tray, he breakfasted comfortably in the living-room. A copy of *The Times* had been thrust through his letter-box. Who had had the thoughtfulness to order it for him he did not know, but he sat on, reading it, for some time, then returned to the kitchen, rinsed the crockery that he had used under the tap, went upstairs, shaved and had a shower and got dressed. By then it was half past nine and he was not sure what to do with himself next.

The obvious thing seemed to be to go for a walk. The morning was fine, the sky cloudless, and it was already warm enough to promise that later the day might become very hot. An expedition to the village to see what shops, if any, were there, and to buy in some supplies for the week-end, as his cold chicken would not last for ever, seemed a good idea. Or perhaps he might drive into Oxford and indulge some nostalgia. On the other hand, to go walking on the downs seemed attractive and after some minutes of indecision the downs won. He let himself out of the cottage and set off along the lane from which, if he remembered it correctly, he would presently be able to find a path that led straight up on to the low green hills.

He found the path and started up it. The bare chalky soil of it was dusty and white. There were patches of cultivation on the hillside, but most of it was untouched grassland, dotted with a few sheep. Once at the top he could see for miles over meadows, copses and villages until the distance became a soft, blue haze. For some time, as he walked, he simply enjoyed the shining morning and gave hardly a thought to Caroline, or to how long he would be able to go on doing this kind of thing without becoming bored, or to something that had happened the evening before that nagged at his mind, mildly disturbing him, yet which he could not quite remember. Someone, he thought, had said something that had struck him as odd, yet who had said it or what it had been eluded him. In any case, it could not be important. It was annoying, however, to be bothered by it. He did his best to put it out of his mind and to think about Caroline.

But this was not very rewarding. He was fairly sure that he meant next to nothing to her. She liked him well enough, as she always had, but that was hardly satisfying. Yet perhaps it was more than she meant to him. He was not actually sure that he liked her at all. That might change, of course, very rapidly if her feeling for him were to alter, but as things were he could not rid himself of a sense that there was some danger for him in seeing too much of her. The danger of pain, of an old wound being reopened. He was old enough now not to be prepared to rush headlong into distress that might be avoided if only he were sufficiently sensible.

But was that cowardly? And if so, what was wrong with being a coward? And what would be the sensible thing to do at the moment? He rather thought that it might be to tell Nigel and Annabel that he had changed his mind about spending his holiday at Upthorn and to look for some travel agent in Tolcaster who could find some cruise or tour which he might be able to join, even at short notice. By this time he had arrived back at the cottage at about half past eleven. He had had a good walk and was now pleasantly tired and ready for a drink and had made up his mind to go into Tolcaster in the afternoon and look for a travel agent.

But then it occurred to him that he had left his passport in Stillborough. So the first thing that he would have to do would be to return to Stillborough and to do that immediately on having arrived here would be a discourtesy that he did not think that he could bring himself to commit. It looked as if, for a few days at least, he must stay where he was. Accepting this, he poured out some whisky, picked up *The Times* once more and had settled down in the easy chair, wondering if he could possibly tackle the crossword, when someone hammered with the knocker on the door.

He went to open it. Leslie Jay stood there. She was in a green cotton dress which made her look younger and less sophisticated than she had the evening before and there was a touch of diffidence in her smile.

'Are you busy?' she asked. 'Am I a nuisance?'

'I've nothing whatever in the world to do,' he answered, 'and I'm very glad to see you.' He stood aside so that she could step into the room. 'A drink?'

'Thank you.'

'Gin and tonic?' The evening before, as he remembered it, that was what she had drunk.

She repeated, 'Thank you,' and he poured it out for her. Then when he had moved *The Times*, which he had dropped in the easy chair and she had sat down in it, he sat down himself on the narrow and not very comfortable window-seat.

'I've a message from my mother,' she said. 'She wondered if you'd come in for drinks tomorrow morning. It isn't a party, it'll just be us and perhaps Nigel and Caroline and possibly Annabel, if she feels up to it. She does occasionally go out, though sometimes she thinks she will, then changes her mind at the last moment. But I don't really know if any of them will come as I haven't been able to get an answer from them. I tried knocking at the door, but nobody came. I suppose Nigel's in Tolcaster. Saturday, he always says, is the most demanding day at the museum. And I suppose Caroline's shopping or washing her hair or something. I'll try phoning them later. But will you come in any case?'

'Thank you very much,' he said. 'I should love to.'

'We're in that red Victorian house about a quarter of a mile along the lane towards Upthorn. It's called Oakwood and there really is one single old oak tree in the garden.'

He nodded. 'I remember passing it on my way here.'

'I don't believe you've been here since we moved in, have you?' she said. 'Or anyway not while I've been here.'

'I've been only once since Annabel had her stroke,' he said, 'and I stayed in the house, not the cottage. There were some other people renting it then.'

'My parents would have been here then, but it must have

been when I was in America. The shop I work for does a good deal of trade over there and I was sent over to learn a bit about that side of it. I enjoyed it so much, I nearly stayed for good.'

'Why didn't you?' He was beginning to think that after all she was not as young as she looked and the slight shyness that she had seemed to feel when she first came had disappeared. She looked relaxed now and sure of herself.

'I honestly don't quite know,' she answered, 'and I've often felt I made a mistake, coming home. But at the time, for some reason, it seemed the natural thing to do. I suppose I wasn't prepared yet to tear up my roots.'

'You're rather lucky to feel you have some,' he said. 'But you'd stay there if you had the chance again, would you?'

She paused for long enough for it to seem that she was giving the question very serious consideration.

'Yes,' she said. 'Or perhaps no. Oh, I don't know. I think I'm rather a fool about it.'

'Going by what you said yesterday, and now this, it sounds as if anyway you aren't altogether satisfied with what you're doing now.'

'Oh, certainly not!'

'Then why not make a change?'

'Is that what you'd like to do yourself—make a change? Nigel always says you've got yourself into a rut and are perfectly happy there. He rather laughs at you about it.'

'But isn't it what he's done himself? He's worked in the Cantlewell for years and he loves it.'

'Oh no, he doesn't!'

He was startled at what he thought was something almost fierce in her tone, apart from the certainty with which she had spoken. She must have seen the surprise on his face for she smiled as if she were dismissing what she had said.

'Of course, Nigel's a great little old fraud,' she remarked. 'First he deceives himself and then other people. If it weren't for Annabel and the passion she's got for that house and of course his dependence on her, he'd shoot off to London tomorrow. And then perhaps New York. And then Sydney. And then heaven knows where. He'd always be on the move, trying one thing after another. But it's very important to him, you see, to seem to be a success, and the most important thing about being successful is for everyone to see that you've achieved whatever it was that you aimed at and that you're wonderfully pleased with it. So even if you aren't really pleased, you pretend that you are.'

'You seem to know him very well,' Gavin said.

'Oh, I do!'

'I believe you might even be right about him, though it's never occurred to me before. Perhaps there's more of our father in him than I've ever thought. But I think you're wrong about one thing. I don't think it's any dependence on Annabel, if you mean financial dependence, that's kept him here, though I suppose there are a lot of people who think it must be.'

'Oh, it isn't?' Her smile was quizzical. 'Are you sure of that?'

'Pretty sure.'

'I realize, of course, that she was very beautiful when she was younger.'

'She was.'

'Are you fond of her?'

'Well, yes, I think so. I suppose so. It's something I've always rather taken for granted.'

'I've an idea you take a lot of things for granted and that's how you manage to be as contented as you are. About what she said yesterday evening . . .'

Suddenly he knew what was coming. It was the small thing that had disturbed him while he was walking on the downs, but which he had not been able to remember. Not that it seemed important to him now that he had done so.

'It was about her first husband,' Leslie said. 'She said he married another woman who was a Catholic and very moral. But would a very moral Catholic have married a divorced man?'

'Possibly not,' he replied. 'But you know you mustn't take Annabel too seriously. It's possible, isn't it, that this woman, whoever she was, wasn't as moral as all that? And it's possible that she wasn't even a Catholic. And it's possible that she never really existed.'

'Do you really mean that?' She gave him a puzzled look. 'That she didn't exist?'

'Oh, I think she probably did, but Annabel does let her imagination run away with her sometimes. Of course, if what she said was true, it's a little difficult to explain.'

She nodded thoughtfully. 'I wonder what happened to the man. I mean, is he alive or dead? Do you think she really doesn't know that?'

'I don't know why she should. It's a very long time since they broke up.'

'I suppose so. I just feel that if I'd ever really cared for someone myself . . . Do you think she really did care for him in the beginning? Don't you think, from the way she described him, he must have had terrific glamour? And if she was very young, you'd think that would have meant a fearful lot to her.'

'Mightn't that have been why she blotted him out so completely when he left her?'

'It was he who left her, was it, not she him?'

'I honestly don't know. It isn't a thing I've thought much about.'

'As, indeed, why should you?' She laughed, finished her drink and stood up. 'I'm shockingly curious about people. It's probably a bad habit. But you're coming in to see us tomorrow, aren't you? Come about twelve o'clock.'

'Thank you very much.'

He opened the door for her and she stepped out into the sunshine.

Returning to the easy chair, he picked up *The Times* from the floor where he had dropped it and once more tried to fix his attention on the crossword. What about 'showy transvestism' in four letters? That ought to be easy, but his mind had gone irritatingly blank. He sometimes caught himself nowadays unable to remember perfectly ordinary words that he was in the habit of using almost daily. He would start on a sentence, quite sure of what he wanted to say, then half way through it would find that he had lost the thread and be unable to finish it. Just commonplace absent-mindedness, he supposed, and not to be worried about once you were past forty, but it was irritating. He had just dropped *The Times* on the floor again and was getting up to pour himself another drink when the telephone rang.

That would be Nigel, he thought, or possibly Caroline, as no one else, unless it was one of the Jays, had his number. But it was unlikely to be a call from the Jays, since they must know that Leslie was coming to deliver their invitation. Of course, they might want to catch her and tell her to make some change in the arrangement that she had made with him. He picked up the telephone.

A voice that he knew spoke immediately. 'Gavin—it's Helena.'

His sister Helena. His heart sank. But how did she know that he was here? Who had told her?

'Yes, it's me,' he said. 'Hallo.'

'Gavin, are you all right?' the voice asked quickly. 'You don't sound quite yourself.'

'Thank you, Helena. I'm quite all right. How are you?'

'Oh, I'm fine. There's never anything wrong with me. When did you get to Upthorn?'

'Yesterday. But how did you know I was here?'

'Well, I tried ringing you at your Stillborough number and couldn't get any answer, so when I'd tried several times I rang that nice landlord of yours and he said he thought you'd gone to stay with your brother, so then I tried ringing Nigel, but it seems he was out and Caroline answered and she told me you were in the cottage and gave me your number. You're meaning to stay on for some time, aren't you? I know your school holidays have started, so that's why I thought we might be able to get in touch.'

'I'm a bit uncertain about my plans,' Gavin said cautiously. 'I may be staying only a few days.'

'That's odd.' She sounded put out. 'Caroline gave me the impression, the distinct impression, that you'd be there for the rest of August at least.'

'I might be. On the other hand, I've a certain itch to go abroad. Italy, perhaps. I haven't been to Italy for a long time. But I haven't really made up my mind.'

'Italy,' she said thoughtfully. 'That would be rather expensive, wouldn't it?'

'Not so terribly.'

'Oh, I know *you* could afford it, but what I was thinking . . . You see, I had what I thought was a rather marvellous idea. I've been feeling very alone recently, I couldn't tell you why, it's just something that happens to me sometimes. I think it's a kind of staleness, a need for a change. And so I thought I might join you at the cottage for two or three weeks.'

Italy at once acquired a very definite attraction.

'That's nice of you, Helena,' he said, 'but I can't honestly say how long I'll be here. Perhaps just for the weekend.'

'Of course, we could go to Italy together, only I'm not sure if I could afford it. How are you thinking of going? By car?'

He knew that she did not like long car journeys. 'I expect so.'

But he had misjudged it this time. 'And staying at lots of little out of the way inns on the way. That does sound rather nice. But perhaps you've already arranged to go with some friend and I'd only be in the way.'

He wished that he was better than he was at telling a downright lie.

'Actually, no. It's just that it's all a bit uncertain still.'

'Is that because . . . ?' She paused.

'Because?' he inquired.

'Oh, I was just wondering if you and Nigel had fallen out or anything like that. I'm sure Caroline thinks you'll be staying at Upthorn for some time. Has there been any trouble between you and Nigel?'

'Absolutely none at all. Why should there be?'

'Because Nigel, as we all know, can be very difficult. If your ideas are a little different from his he can be shockingly unkind about it. He's such a sceptic about things he really doesn't understand in the least, and he doesn't care how much he hurts your feelings. I've done my very best to keep on good terms with him, but sometimes it's been almost more than I could bring myself to do.'

'Then would it be such a good idea for you to come here? You couldn't avoid seeing a good deal of him.'

'I've been wondering if we might get on a little better than we have in the past. Suffering does soften people and he must have suffered quite a lot in the last year or two. He has suffered, I suppose? I mean, what's happened to Annabel does matter to him?'

'Very much, I should think.'

'He isn't simply indifferent to it? He doesn't just think of it as a fearful inconvenience?'

'I'm sure he doesn't.'

'Because he is so selfish. How is she, by the way?'

If he had been more certain about this than he was he would have found it easier to answer.

'It's difficult to say exactly,' he said. 'She's slightly paralysed still, I think, but hates it if anyone notices it, and she's . . .' He hesitated.

'She's what?' Helena asked with what sounded like a kind of eagerness in her voice.

'Oh, I'd say very unhappy at her limitations,' he replied evasively.

'I thought you were going to say a bit—well, unstable. But then she's always been that, or so it seemed to me. Do you think there's a chance that I might be able to help her at all, Gavin?'

'Just how do you mean?'

'Well, I have helped people, you know. Quite a lot of people. You'd be surprised at the letters I sometimes get. I've a certain power . . . Not very much of one, perhaps, and I don't know where it comes from and I feel very humble about it, and I know you don't believe in it for a moment, but don't you think it might at least be worth trying? I mean, if only you'd stay on at the cottage for a time I could join you. It doesn't sound as if you've any very definite plans about Italy.'

His plans about Italy became very definite at that moment.

'It's very good of you, Helena, and I'm sure Annabel will be very grateful for the thought,' he said, 'but I can't promise anything at the moment. Suppose you ring up again in another day or two.'

With luck, by the time that she did, he might be on his way back to Stillborough to collect his passport.

'I can't help the feeling that something's wrong between you and Nigel,' she said. 'Be honest with me, Gavin. It is, isn't it?'

'Absolutely not a thing, I swear it.'

'After all, we've all of us always quarrelled so much. We've never been an affectionate family. You're the only

one in it I ever feel I can talk to at all. I'd like to spend a
little time with you. But I'll ring back sometime soon and
find out what you're really going to do. Goodbye, Gavin.'

'Goodbye, Helena.'

He put the telephone down, sure all at once that he had
been unnecessarily unwelcoming, really quite unkind, even
downright brutal. It was how she nearly always made him
feel and it always made him feel ashamed of himself, but
did not prevent it happening again next time. The truth
was that he was quite fond of Helena but simply could not
stand much of her company. If there was any risk that she
might descend on him here he must make up his mind
quickly about what to do.

It took him only a few minutes to decide to go across to
the house opposite and find out if Nigel had yet returned
for his lunch. He could talk the matter over with him.
Opening the door of the living-room, he stepped out into
the courtyard and it was just as he did so that the door of
the house opened and a stout, elderly man came out. He
came out extremely quickly and let the door slam shut behind him. Except that he was rather too stout and too elderly
for it, it might almost have been said that he was running.
Certainly he was in a great hurry as he made for the grey
Mercedes that was parked just inside the gate.

That Gavin had not seen the car arrive might have been
due to the fact that when it had done so he had been talking
on the telephone with his back to the window, or perhaps
it had been when he was sitting on the window-seat, talking
to Leslie. It could not have been any earlier than that because there had been no car in the courtyard when he returned from his walk on the downs. The man clambered
into the car and, accelerating at once, took it in a wild
sweep round the rose-bed, out of the gate and away down
the lane. He gave no sign of having seen Gavin, but he had
seen the man's large, plump face as he shot past. He looked

exceedingly angry. Angry or frightened. It is sometimes difficult to tell the two states apart.

Gavin wondered if this could perhaps be Oliver, who knew about guns. But if so, what could have happened in the house to upset him so badly? As far as Gavin had seen, no one had been at the door to let him out. He appeared to have wrenched it open on his own and let it slam shut behind him as he fled. But someone other than Annabel, who did not answer doors, must have been in the house to let him in. Gavin strolled across the courtyard and hammered on the door with the iron knocker.

No one came even when he had tried knocking three times. But someone must be there, or how had the man got in? It was possible, Gavin supposed, that Caroline might be sitting out on the terrace and if she were might not have heard him at the door. Starting off to look for her, he walked to the end of the house and turned on to the terrace, but saw no one sitting there. However, he saw that the door that opened on to it from the drawing-room was open and going up the two steps that led on to it, he went to the door.

He had taken only one step into the room when he stood still, his heart giving a sickening beat. Disbelief, anxiety and concern all seemed to explode inside him at the same moment. Annabel lay on the floor. Except that she was lying on her back, not on her face, she looked very much as she had looked the evening before when she had tripped over the edge of the carpet and fallen. Even the gun was there as it had been then, lying within reach of one outflung hand. She was quite still and very white.

Gavin had had very little to do with death during his life. He had been too young to remember much about his mother's and he had been at Oxford when his father had died in Australia. He had been born after the war and had known nothing of its violence and terror, even as a childish memory. But he was certain that Annabel was dead.

He walked towards her, treading softly as if his footsteps could disturb her. Bending down, he looked at her expressionless face, then gently put the back of his hand against her cheek. It was quite warm. Whatever had happened to her, it could not have been more than a short time ago. It must have been a second stroke, he supposed.

Just for one fearful instant he had an impulse to flee from the scene like the stout, elderly man whom he had seen running away from the house. For this must have been what the man had been fleeing from. So he could not have been Oliver Penbury, for he was a doctor and would not have run away, panic-stricken, from death. But what had Annabel been doing with the gun this morning?

And where was Caroline?

Gavin walked round the fallen body and out into the hall. 'Caroline!' he called out. 'Caroline!'

There was a curious smell in the air, an unpleasant smell as if of something burning. He thought that it was coming from the kitchen and the thought, foolishly inappropriate at such a time, crossed his mind that it might be some experiment in cookery of Caroline's going wrong, as he could imagine things often did. But if that was what it was, if it was something boiling over in the kitchen which she had forgotten about, it probably meant that she was upstairs.

He called again, 'Caroline!'

The sound of his voice seemed to echo in an empty house.

He thought of going upstairs to look for her, for surely she would not have been so absent-minded as to leave the house when she had left something cooking on the stove. Yet people sometimes do do such things. He went quickly through the dining-room to the kitchen to turn the stove off before he went upstairs to look for her.

He had no need to go upstairs. Caroline was in the kitchen. She was sitting at the table in the middle of the room, fallen forward over a cookery book that she appeared to have been reading. There was not a great deal of blood, but one side of her face was thickly smeared with it and a dark hole gaped in her temple.

He was alone in the house with two dead women.

Something that might have been Irish stew sizzled and spat on the stove and smelled horribly.

CHAPTER 4

How Gavin managed to get from the kitchen to the telephone in the hall he was never able afterwards to remember. But there he was, dialling the number of the museum in Tolcaster, which he had found on a pad beside the telephone. A woman's voice answered him and he asked for Nigel. His voice was hoarse and he was shivering. The woman told him that Mr Cleaver had already left for home. How long ago, he asked. She replied that she was not sure but believed that he must arrive there soon. Could she take a message? He thanked her but said no and put the telephone down. It was strange that the shivering seemed to be entirely internal, for he could see that the hand that had held the telephone was quite steady.

For a little while, he did not know for how long, he stayed where he was, staring blankly at the wall in front of him. To go back to the kitchen or to the drawing-room seemed impossible. He had a feeling that he ought to telephone the police. But at the same time he felt that it would be better to wait to do this until Nigel had arrived. Suddenly he made up his mind what to do. He pushed the front door open and went running out to where he had left his car, tumbled into it and drove out through the gate and along the lane towards Upthorn, swinging in through the gates of the big, square, red brick Victorian house that was only about a quarter of a mile along it.

Stopping with a jerk in front of the white-painted front door, he rang the bell beside it and heard it peal inside the house. The door was opened almost immediately by Marion Jay. She was in a flowered cotton dress with an apron tied round her waist. She smiled but looked a little surprised to see him.

'Oh, Mr Cleaver—Gavin—?' she said. 'How nice to see you. Come in.' Then at something that she saw in his face, she added quickly, 'Is something wrong?'

He immediately found himself tongue-tied. He could not think why he had come here instead of telephoning from the Cleavers' house. He would almost certainly have found the Jays' number on the pad beside the telephone. His voice came out as hoarsely now as it had when he had tried to telephone Nigel at the Cantlewell.

'Is Dr Jay in?' he asked. 'Can I see him?'

'I'm sorry, he's out on call and I don't know when he'll be back,' she answered. 'But please come in. Something is wrong, isn't it?'

'No, thank you, I won't come in, I ought to be getting back,' he said. 'I oughtn't really to have come.'

He was beginning to feel that what had brought him had been a desperate desire to get out of that other house, not unlike what the man whom he had seen fleeing from it must have been feeling. But he was beginning to feel a little more like himself now.

'I must get back,' he said.

'Is it Annabel?' she asked, her tone kind and anxious. 'It is, isn't it?'

'Yes, and—and there's other trouble too. I can't really tell you . . . I mean, I haven't really taken it in yet, but Caroline . . . I can't believe it, but she's dead. I think she's been shot. I hoped Dr Jay could come—'

She interrupted him. 'Shot? Caroline shot?'

'That's what it looks like,' he said. 'Of course, perhaps I'm wrong, but Annabel's lying in the drawing-room, as if she'd collapsed there, and I think she's dead too, and she's holding a gun—I think it's that gun she showed us yesterday evening—no, I don't mean she's holding it, it's just lying beside her, but it looks as if she'd been holding it and it fell out of her hand when she collapsed.'

'Are you trying to tell me you think she shot Caroline?' Though there was horrified shock on Marion's face, her voice was much firmer than Gavin's.

'Perhaps—I don't know—yes, that's how it looks,' he said.

She put out a hand and grasped him by the arm, pulling him inside.

'Just a minute,' she said. 'I'm going to phone Oliver. He'll be at the surgery in the village this morning. I'll tell him to meet us at the house. Then I'll go back with you.'

She was undoing her apron as she spoke, dropping it on a chair in the hall, then she shot into a room that opened off it and Gavin heard the tinkle of a telephone as she picked it up. He heard her speaking briefly, then she reappeared.

'He says he can be there pretty soon,' she said. 'Now let's go.'

They went out together to the car and Gavin drove back, feeling quite sure that he ought not to have come. He ought never to have left the house, for of course he should have been there to meet Nigel and give him some warning of what he was going to have to face. Even if it did not help much, he could at least have been spared walking in on it as unprepared as Gavin had been himself.

However, Nigel's car was not in the courtyard when he and Marion Jay arrived. He had not got home yet.

Gavin took her in by the door on to the terrace. He had realized that her nerve was far better than his own, but when she saw Annabel he heard her give a sharp gasp, then saw her become rigidly still before taking a few steps forward and standing looking down at the dead woman on the floor.

'I don't understand,' she said after a moment. 'The gun—why the gun?'

'If you can face it, come into the kitchen and see,' Gavin said.

'It's the one she showed us last night—I suppose it is.'

'I think so.'

'But why? Why did she—well, use it?'

'Perhaps we'll never know that.'

'I mean, there didn't seem to be anything wrong with her mind, did there? I know she could be sort of slow sometimes, taking things in, but never anything to worry one. Oh, poor Annabel, what happened to you?' She stooped and touched Annabel's pale gold hair with a gesture of great tenderness.

'If you'd sooner not come into the kitchen, I'll telephone the police now,' Gavin said. 'There isn't really any reason why you should have to go in there.'

Her strength had helped to calm him. He had not yet begun to take in what the death of Caroline meant to him.

Marion turned towards the door.

'I'd better see, hadn't I? If you like, I'll telephone the police. I know Inspector Frost a little. You needn't come in yourself if you can't bear it.'

She walked across the hall, through the dining-room and into the kitchen.

Gavin stayed at her heels and again heard her gasp, but this time she did not advance into the room, but stayed only just inside the door with a look as much of incredulity as of shock on her face. Then suddenly her nerve seemed to fail her, for she covered her face with her hands, wheeled and stumbled out of the kitchen, blundering against Gavin as she went. In the hall she stood still again, let her hands fall and stood there, breathing deeply. At that moment Gavin heard a key in the door and Nigel came in.

Looking from one to the other, he seemed to sense at once that there was something very seriously wrong and a strange look of fear appeared on his face.

'Annabel!' he said at once. 'Something's happened to her!'

Gavin realized then that for a long time Nigel must have been living with the fear that Annabel had only been living on borrowed time, that at any time she might have a second stroke that would kill her and that the presence there just then of Gavin and Marion, with the looks that were on their faces, told him that this had happened. Some unconscious glance or gesture of Gavin's must have told him where to go, for he plunged straight into the drawing-room.

Gavin and Marion waited in the hall. A long time seemed to pass, though it was only in fact a few minutes, then Nigel came out. Except for the pallor of his handsome face, it showed very little.

'Desmond isn't here?' he said to Marion.

'No, he's out on call this morning,' she said. 'I couldn't get him. But I've phoned Oliver. He'll be here any time now.'

'Not that there's anything he can do,' Nigel said. 'Of course, I've known this would probably happen sometime, but that doesn't help much. How did you find her?'

'I came in through the door on to the terrace,' Gavin replied. 'There were things I wanted to talk over with you. It doesn't matter what they were, they aren't important. And I found her, and then . . . Nigel, there's something else we've got to show you. It's Caroline—'

'What's wrong with Caroline?' Nigel interrupted sharply.

'God, I don't know how to tell you this,' Gavin said, 'but

she's in the kitchen, and she's—she's dead too, Nigel. It looks as if she's been shot. She's sitting at the table and—'

But he got no further, for Nigel strode past him into the dining-room and through it into the kitchen. Gavin was about to follow him, but Marion put a hand on his arm and held him in the hall.

After another minute or two Nigel reappeared. He looked more dazed than he had when he came out of the drawing-room, as if the shock had been greater. His face had a yellowish pallor. It was as if he did not see either of the two of them, standing there. When he spoke, his voice was unnaturally high.

'We must call the police,' he said. 'They'll have to know about this. Even if it's obvious Annabel didn't know what she was doing, they'll have to go through the routine. A post-mortem. An inquest. The press. Death of noted novelist, was she a murderess? . . .' Suddenly he made for the stairs and darted up them. The sound of someone violently retching, probably vomiting, reached Gavin from the bathroom above.

'I'll telephone,' Marion said and fairly quickly succeeded in being connected with an Inspector Frost, told him that there had been a fatal accident at the house in Upthorn and that she thought that it was urgent that the police should be informed.

As she put the telephone down again, she said, 'They're sending someone. I'll stay, shall I, or shall I just be in the way?'

'Please stay,' Gavin said.

'There's not much I can do to help, but if I can . . .' She went into the dining-room, drew a chair out from the table and dropped down on to it. 'I wonder where they keep their brandy. I could do with some and you look as if you could too.'

Gavin remembered that there was brandy in a sideboard

in the dining-room. There were glasses there too. He filled two, then as Nigel came into the room, filled a third, sat down at the table and, as he sipped his, thought suddenly that none of them had had any lunch and most likely were not going to have any. He remembered the Irish stew that had been cooking in the kitchen and thought with surprise at himself that he must have switched off the ring under it before he left the kitchen to telephone Nigel, an entirely automatic action of which he had no memory.

'I tried to telephone you at the museum to tell you what had happened,' he said to Nigel, 'but you'd left already.'

Nigel had not sat down. He stood, holding the brandy but not tasting it. He seemed to Gavin to have become strangely gaunt. The skin of his face seemed to have shrunk against the bone behind it. But he had an air of restless energy, as if he felt that there was something that he ought to be doing and was angry with himself because he did not know what it was. That air of energy, of vitality, which even at a time like this had not left him, was one of the things that had always made him attractive to many people.

'You said Oliver's coming,' he said to Marion.

'Yes,' she said.

'And you've phoned the police? Of course I ought to have done that, but for the moment . . . All the same, thank you. I suppose she must have done it—Annabel, I mean.'

'Shot Caroline?' Marion said.

Abruptly Nigel swallowed half the brandy in his glass, then gave a convulsive shudder. 'Well, didn't she?'

'It's how it looks,' Marion said.

'That affair with the gun last night—it ought to have warned us.' Nigel walked to the window and stood looking out, as if he were watching for the arrival of Oliver Penbury. 'It wasn't normal. Of course, I knew she had a gun, but I'd quite forgotten about it. I'd even forgotten where she kept it till I saw her suddenly making for that bureau.

It just happens that I hardly ever looked in it. That drawer's got the sort of documents in it one keeps for years but never looks at. Our birth certificates, our insurance policy, our old passports, you know the sort of thing. We've lots of old passports in there. You know how they send the old one back to you with one corner cut off when you get a new one. I don't know how many we've got. And I should think our most recent ones are out of date. Of course we haven't been abroad since she got ill, though we used to travel a good deal. And I shouldn't be surprised if she herself had forgotten the gun was in there till something someone said last night reminded her of it. She was talking about Jerome Halliday, wasn't she?' He broke off. 'Here's Oliver.'

Swallowing the rest of his brandy, he put the glass down and went to the door.

Oliver Penbury was not in the least like what Gavin had been expecting. He could not have said why, but he had been assuming that the doctor would be about the same age as Desmond Jay, a stolid, reliable-looking man, not unlike his partner. Not that there was any reason to think that he looked unreliable, but he was many years younger than Desmond Jay, perhaps only a year or two over thirty, with a round face with a short, upturned nose, bright blue eyes under thick, sandy eyebrows and untidy, reddish, curly hair. He was wearing dark green corduroy trousers and a brown pullover. He was tall and well-built. Though there was a look of professional concern on his face, he seemed unable to stop himself giving Marion a smile of friendly greeting.

'Marion told me you've got trouble here,' he said, 'and Des is out.'

'She didn't tell you more than that?' Nigel said.

'Not really. Something about Annabel and a gun and that it was urgent. I know Marion wouldn't have said it was urgent if it wasn't, so I didn't really wait to take it in.

She hasn't—I mean, Annabel hasn't—well, shot herself, has she?'

'It doesn't look like it,' Nigel said. He had grown noticeably calmer since the young man had arrived. 'Come into the drawing-room. You'd better see her first.'

'*First?*' Oliver Penbury exclaimed. 'You don't mean . . . ? What do you mean, Nigel?'

'That there are two of them,' Nigel answered. 'But come and look at Annabel first.'

He grasped Penbury by the arm and steered him into the drawing-room.

They were not in there for long. When they reappeared Nigel took the other man straight into the kitchen and they did not stay there long either. When they returned to the dining-room a gravity which somehow did now seem to suit it had settled on Penbury's face.

'And you just walked in and found this?' he said to Nigel.

'No, my brother did,' Nigel answered. It only occurred to him then that he had not introduced Gavin and the doctor to one another. 'This is my brother, who's staying in the cottage. Oliver Penbury, Gavin. He came in and . . . Gavin, you said you came because there was something you wanted to talk over with me. What was it?'

'As I said, it's nothing important,' Gavin said. 'It can wait. It just happened that I came over and . . .' He hit his forehead with a knuckle. 'How could I have forgotten a thing like that? Just as I was leaving the cottage a man came out of your door, practically running, let the door slam shut behind him and made for a car that was just inside the gate and drove off. Were you expecting anyone this morning?'

'A man?' Nigel said. 'What kind of man?'

'An oldish, rather stout one. In his late sixties, I should say, and bald and wearing a dark suit and looking in quite a state.'

'What kind of car?' Penbury asked, as if this were more important than what the man had been like.

'A grey Mercedes,' Gavin said.

Penbury looked at Nigel. 'Does that suggest anyone special to you?'

'Offhand, I can't think of anyone I know with a Mercedes,' Nigel said. 'Did you notice the number, Gavin?'

'I'm sorry, no,' Gavin replied. 'All I really noticed about him was that he drove off like a madman and looked as if he were in a hell of a rage about something. A rage, or perhaps he was just frightened. That's what I'm inclined now to think he was. If he'd come in and found what I did, you can understand he might be in a hurry to get away.'

'Who let him in?' Penbury asked.

'Perhaps no one,' Gavin said. 'Perhaps he came in as I did through the door on to the terrace. Doesn't he sound like anyone you know, Nigel?'

Nigel shook his head. 'I can't think of anyone at the moment. If perhaps it was someone who wanted to interview Annabel ... But if it was, it's hardly likely he'd have arrived unexpectedly, and whoever he was, it's what he must have done, or she'd have said something about it to me. And he found her lying collapsed on the floor in the drawing-room. But why should he have panicked and bolted?'

'Perhaps because of the gun beside her,' Marion suggested. 'If he didn't look at her closely, he may have thought it was suicide and been anxious not to get involved. Of course, if he'd gone into the kitchen and found Caroline, it's understandable he might have wanted to get away before anyone came. But why should he have gone to the kitchen?'

'It just could have been because of a rather awful smell of burning stew,' Gavin said. 'I noticed it when I went into the hall, and it was partly why I went in myself.'

'Or if he heard a shot . . .' Penbury began, then paused. 'I wonder if that could be possible. I mean, that as he came into the drawing-room, he heard a shot in the kitchen and rushed in to see what had happened, saw Annabel standing over Caroline with the gun in her hand and she turned it on him and that's why he bolted for his life. Then she went to the drawing-room and the shock of what she'd done was too much for her and she collapsed and died herself. That makes a sort of sense, doesn't it?'

'Isn't it possible that it was Caroline who shot herself?' Marion said.

They all looked at her. She gave a frown, as if she were trying to think something out.

'There's been something odd about her ever since she came here, hasn't there?' she said. 'Giving up her part in that soap-opera, possibly giving up her career altogether, staying here looking after Annabel—we all thought how good of her it was, particularly as the sort of life she was leading here really didn't seem to suit her. Don't you think there could have been some tragedy in her life that she was running away from, or perhaps even hiding from, and when she found out yesterday evening where the gun was kept, she decided to use it on herself? That seems to me more likely than that Annabel murdered her.'

'Then how did the gun get into the drawing-room, beside Annabel?' Penbury asked.

'Annabel could have heard the shot and gone to see what had happened,' Marion said, 'and taken the gun almost without thinking of what she was doing and gone to the drawing-room and come face to face with the stranger who'd just come in and he thought she was pointing the gun at him and fled for his life. And then, as you said, the shock of it all was too much for her and that second stroke we've all been afraid of happened and she died.'

There was a moment's silence, then Nigel nodded.

'It could have happened like that. It does make better sense than that Annabel suddenly took to murder. Gavin, did you hear a shot?'

'No,' Gavin said.

'Are you sure?'

'Yes, but you see, I was talking on the telephone,' Gavin said. 'If it happened just as the telephone started ringing I probably wouldn't have heard anything, and even if it was while I was just talking I don't suppose I'd have paid any attention to it.' He moved towards the window. 'Marion, I think your friend, Inspector Frost, is just arriving.'

Detective-Inspector Raymond Frost, attended by Detective-Constable Crewe, arrived at the front door and were let in by Nigel. The Detective-Inspector was about forty, a tall man, broad-shouldered and strongly built, who held himself very erect, had dark, bushy hair growing low on his forehead and dark eyes spaced far apart in a broad, ruddy face. The constable was a much younger man, perhaps about thirty, also tall but with an air of casualness about him, an untidiness about his fair hair, a shabbiness about the not very well-fitting suit that he was wearing, which made him look almost boyish.

The Inspector spoke to Marion Jay. 'Good morning, Mrs Jay. It was you who rang me, wasn't it? An accident, you said, a fatal accident.'

She had stood up when he entered.

'Yes, Mr Frost, I telephoned and that seemed the easiest thing to say, but it may not have been—well, altogether accurate.' She introduced him to Nigel and Gavin. The Inspector and Oliver Penbury had evidently met before, for they greeted each other with brief nods. She went on, 'Mr Cleaver will show you what's actually happened. Nigel?' She looked at him questioningly and he nodded and gestured to the two detectives to follow him.

They went into the drawing-room, were there for a short

time, then Nigel led them into the kitchen. They were there for longer and when they came out again there had been a subtle change in them both, a change which Gavin thought of as a cruious increase in professionalism. When they had first come in they had been merely two men entering a strange house prepared to encounter tragedy and probably to sympathize. Now they were two policemen with the weight of authority on their shoulders.

Frost addressed Gavin. 'Mr Cleaver tells me it was you who discovered what had happened here.'

'Yes,' Gavin said.

'What time was that?'

'I'm not sure,' Gavin said. 'I think it was around twelve o'clock.'

'You realize, of course, that the one thing it couldn't have been was an accident. It was murder or suicide. Mr Cleaver has suggested to me that Miss Astor's death could have been suicide. It's just possible.'

'That was my suggestion, Mr Frost,' Marion said. 'It seems to me more probable than that Mrs Cleaver could have killed her sister.'

'Her half-sister, Mr Cleaver told me,' Frost said.

'Does that make much difference?' Marion asked.

'Perhaps none at all. And Mrs Cleaver's own death could have been natural, brought on by shock. But what we shall need to know is whether Miss Astor's fingerprints are on the gun. If she killed herself they should be there, as well as Mrs Cleaver's. I'll have to send for the fingerprint people, the photographers and so on. The telephone's in the hall, isn't it?'

'And if my sister-in-law's fingerprints aren't on the gun . . .' Nigel said and stopped.

'We'll go into that when we know,' Frost said, walked out to the hall and started telephoning.

The constable stayed in the dining-room and though he

looked as casual as ever, with his hands in his pockets, Gavin found himself suddenly thinking that the man had remained there to watch them. It was not his first encounter with the police. Boys at Stillborough sometimes did crazy things, as adolescent boys will, and he had been called in once or twice to take responsibility for them, but he had never yet been a witness when what was probably a serious crime had been committed. When Frost returned to the dining-room he addressed Gavin once more.

'Are you staying in this house, Mr Cleaver?'

'No, I'm staying in the cottage over there,' Gavin said, nodding towards the window.

'Since when?'

'Yesterday morning.'

'Where do you live?'

'In Stillborough. I teach at Stillborough College.'

'And you didn't come over here this morning at all until about twelve o'clock?'

'That's correct.'

'Did you happen to see anything of Mrs Cleaver or Miss Astor before that?'

'No, I went for a fairly long walk on the downs and soon after I got back I had a visit from Miss Jay, who stayed talking for a short time. It was a little after she left that I came over.'

'My daughter, Mr Frost,' Marion said. 'I sent her over to invite Mr Gavin Cleaver for drinks tomorrow morning. She was also to invite Mr and Mrs Nigel Cleaver, but I don't know if she saw anyone here.'

'She told me she'd knocked at the door and got no reply,' Gavin said, 'but that she'd phone them later.'

'And that would have been when?' Frost asked. 'Half past eleven, quarter to twelve?'

'Something like that,' Gavin said. 'Soon after she left I had a telephone call from a sister of mine and it was after that that I came over. But an odd thing happened just as I was coming. The door here opened and a man came running out. There was a grey Mercedes parked just inside the gate and he practically tumbled into it and drove off as if the devil was after him.'

'Leaving the door behind him open?'

'No, it had slammed shut. When I knocked, nobody came, so I went round to the terrace and came into the drawing-room and found—well, you know what I found.'

'Can you describe the man?'

'I should think he was in his sixties, rather stout, fairly bald. I can't remember much about his clothes except that he was wearing a dark suit, I think.'

'It would be too much to hope that you noticed the number of the car,' Frost said.

'I'm afraid it would,' Gavin agreed.

Frost looked round the room. 'Does Mr Cleaver's description mean anything to any of you?'

Heads were shaken. There was silence.

'Well, I shall want to talk to you again presently, Mr Cleaver,' Frost said to Gavin, 'but I think it might be best if you'd go over to the cottage now and wait for me there. A number of men will soon be arriving here and there isn't all that much room. Mrs Jay, if you want to go home, there's no reason why you shouldn't. We can find you there later, I assume.'

'Of course,' she said.

'Will your daughter be at home too?'

'Probably.'

She went to the door and stepped out into the courtyard. Gavin followed her.

She stayed at his side as he went towards the cottage and when they reached the door he invited her in. She hesitated, began by saying that she ought to be getting home as she had to tell Desmond and Leslie what had happened and that she should be getting the lunch, though Desmond had perhaps helped himself already as he had a cricket match to go to, then she changed her mind and went into the cottage with Gavin. But she would not sit down.

'I mustn't stay for more than a moment,' she said, 'but about that idea of mine that Caroline could have killed herself, I wanted to ask you, you don't think much of it, do you, Gavin?'

'I don't know,' he answered. 'It's possible, I think.'

'You see, I've felt sure ever since she came here that there was something wrong in her life. I mean, giving up her career just when she was becoming successful, it was odd, wasn't it?'

'Yes, I've been puzzled by it too,' Gavin agreed.

'But you don't know of anything special yourself?'

'No, I've seen very little of her for a long time.'

'But you knew her well.'

'I'm not sure.'

'I think I know what you mean. But weren't you and she once engaged to be married? I know it's impertinent to ask, but Annabel hinted at it.'

He shook his head. 'Not really. Nearly, perhaps, but anyway it didn't work out.'

'Why do you think she really stayed here?' There was anxiety in her tone and she was watching him intently. 'Did it never strike you as strange?'

He moved away from her so that she could not look at him too closely.

'Wasn't it just to look after Annabel?' he said. 'Does there have to be any other reason?'

'I think there was. I'm sure there was.'

'You're thinking of that tragedy there may have been in her life, or that she may have been running away from something.'

'Or someone.'

'Did she strike you as someone who was afraid of anything?'

'No, but then . . .' She raised her hands a little, then dropped them in a gesture that was oddly forlorn. 'I mean, one knows so little about other people, even the people one's supposed to know best. Don't most of us have fears we do our best to hide?'

Remembering that look that Desmond Jay had given Caroline during dinner the evening before, Gavin thought that he knew what one of her fears was. Yet that glance might have meant almost nothing. It had probably been no more than a momentary sense of attraction to a woman who was used to attracting many others besides himself. And Caroline had not responded to it. She had been aware of it, Gavin had been sure, but if anything it had amused her. That was a new thought for him and it gave him a moment of sharp discomfort, for whatever she had failed to feel about him, he had always been sure that she had taken him seriously and after her fashion had been pained at what she had done to him.

'I suppose,' Marion went on, 'that Annabel left her a good deal of money.'

'I don't know,' Gavin replied.

'After all, they were sisters and Annabel owed her a great deal for having given up her career just to look after her.'

'And you think that might have been one of the reasons why Caroline came here?'

'Oh, I don't mean that,' Marion said quickly. 'After all, Annabel might have lived for years. I was just wondering whom it will go to now.'

'I should think to Nigel.'

'Even if Caroline left a will, leaving it to someone else?'

He wondered what she could be thinking of now, for it could hardly be of her husband.

'Would she have inherited anything if she'd died before

Annabel?' he asked. 'If it turns out to be true that Annabel shot her and then died herself, I don't believe Caroline would have inherited anything from her.'

'No—no, of course not. I'm in such a muddle. But suppose she'd lived, what do you think she would have done when Annabel died?'

'Gone back to the theatre, I suppose.'

'Do you really think so?'

'I don't know. It's something I haven't thought about.'

'No, of course not. As I said, I'm in a muddle. Do you know, by the way, that Leslie and Oliver are engaged, at least I think they are?' All of a sudden she seemed in a hurry to change the subject. 'It's difficult to be sure about that sort of thing nowadays, isn't it? I mean, she doesn't wear a ring and if you mentioned a trousseau she'd have to go and look up the meaning of the word in a dictionary, and they don't seem to have fixed any date for the marriage. All the same, I think it's what they want. I'm so pleased about it and so is Desmond. He and Oliver are in a group practice in Tolcaster and he knows Oliver very well. There are four of them altogether, with Desmond the senior partner, and if Leslie and Oliver do get married it means they'll be able to stay near us and of course we're very happy about that. Now I must be going home, but I just wanted to say I realize you won't want to come to us for drinks tomorrow morning. In fact, you may not be able to if the police are here, as I dare say they will be. But if you do want to come any time, or if there's anything any of us can do to help, please let us know. Perhaps you ought to have our telephone number.'

She wrote it down on a scrap of paper she found in her handbag, laid it down beside the telephone and left. Gavin dropped into the easy chair and sat there for a time, almost motionless, with his legs stretched out before him, his hands folded on his stomach and his gaze, expressionless except for a kind of intentness in it, as if it were trying to see something a long way off, fixed on the ceiling.

He did not know how long he had been there when it suddenly occurred to him that he was hungry. Or if not hungry, then empty, emotionally and physically. Was that how grief hit one? But he supposed that it would be a good thing to have something to eat, even though there was something repellent about the actual thought of it. Going out to the kitchen, he made a sandwich of what was left of yesterday's cold chicken and a mug of instant coffee and had just taken them into the living-room when there came a knock at the door. Detective-Inspector Frost, he assumed, and was right.

The Inspector stood there without his satellite, DC Crewe, who must have remained at the house, Gavin thought, either to keep watch on its two occupants, Nigel and Oliver Penbury, or to receive the other members of the police force, the fingerprint men, the photographers, the ambulance men, of whom the Inspector had spoken and who must be due to arrive any time now.

'Don't let me interrupt your lunch,' Frost said, seeing the sandwich. 'Times like this, people sometimes forget to eat. Doesn't do any good. Try to behave as normally as possible, then shock may not do as much to you as you expect. That must have been quite a shock you had this morning.'

'It was,' Gavin said. 'Would you care for some coffee?'

'I won't say no to that,' Frost said. 'It's just about what I need.'

Gavin returned to the kitchen and as the kettle was still hot with the water that he had boiled for his own coffee, took only a moment to make a second mugful. When he came back to the living-room he found that Frost was sitting in the easy chair, or rather, sprawling there with his head back and his eyes shut. But hearing Gavin come in, he started pulling himself to his feet.

'Don't get up,' Gavin said and, giving the detective the mug, sat down on the window-seat and started to munch his sandwich.

'I believe I'd have been asleep in another moment,' Frost said and certainly his broad, ruddy face looked very tired. 'Was up most of the night, nothing important, some burglars in an old lady's house, caught all the bastards, no real damage done, but it hasn't left me in the best possible state to deal with the sort of thing you've got here.' He sipped some coffee, grimacing because he found it too hot to swallow. 'What's your idea, now that you've had a little time to think about it? Did she do it?'

'Miss Astor?'

'No, no, Mrs Cleaver. Seems obvious, doesn't it? She had the gun, took it out of the drawer, shot her sister, went to the drawing-room, but by then the shock of what she'd done was too much for her and she collapsed there and died. Straightforward thing if you look at it like that.'

'What did she mean to do with the gun?' Gavin asked. 'Why did she take it into the drawing-room? How did she mean to get rid of it?'

'Perhaps she hadn't got around to thinking about that. I gather she hasn't been quite herself lately. Done a few peculiar things. I heard about what she did yesterday evening, saw that broken window in the dining-room.'

'Yet she'd managed to write two books,' Gavin said. 'You know she's a well-known novelist, don't you?'

'Yes, I've heard about that. Perhaps you can still write books even if you have gone a bit peculiar. Of course, what I'm really interested in is motive. Why should she kill her sister? Anything you can tell me about that?'

'So far as I know, they were on excellent terms.'

'No jealousy, for instance?'

Gavin gave Frost a puzzled look, not sure of his meaning. 'Jealousy? Because of that television success of Miss Astor's, d'you mean? But she's thrown that up. I'd say, of the two, Mrs Cleaver was the more successful.'

'No, no, the husband, that's what I'm asking about,' Frost said impatiently. He gulped some coffee. 'Miss Astor was a good-looking woman, wasn't she? And Mrs Cleaver was a sick one and getting on in age. Living in the house with her and Mr Cleaver, couldn't her sister have got a bit more involved with him than Mrs Cleaver liked?'

Gavin felt that probably he looked very stupid. It startled him that this particular possibility had never crossed his mind. After a moment he shook his head.

'I don't believe my brother ever looked at any woman but his wife,' he said.

'Suppose he didn't, but suppose she thought he did,' Frost said. 'People can be made miserable by jealousy for which there's no foundation.'

'Yes, I know, but I don't think it would have happened in Annabel's case. She was very sure of herself. But of course I realize . . .' Gavin hesitated. 'You'll say again that perhaps she wasn't quite her normal self. For all I know, she may have been suffering from a pathological sort of jealousy. But I don't think so.'

'There's another thing I wanted to ask you about,' Frost went on. 'A thing that strikes me as odd, though perhaps it doesn't mean anything. Mrs Cleaver seems to have made a will only a fortnight ago. It was in the drawer of that bureau in the dining-room where she'd kept the gun. Just a very informal will on one of those forms you can get from the post-office, and it was in there with things like her and her husband's birth certificates, old passports and so on, and it was witnessed by a Beatrice Nevin and a James Boyce and it left her whole estate to Nigel Beresford Cleaver.'

'Nothing to her sister?'

'Nothing at all.'

'Perhaps that's a bit strange, but perhaps it's not really

odd. I don't know who James Boyce is, but Beatrice Nevin is the daily woman who's been working for them for years.'

'Could be it's nothing,' Frost said. 'Only Mrs Cleaver didn't state anywhere that Nigel Beresford Cleaver was her husband. Seems sort of unnatural to me. "I leave the whole of my estate to my beloved husband . . ." I mean, isn't that the sort of thing people usually say? And another thing, in that drawer with all the other documents there doesn't seem to be a marriage certificate, or one of divorce either. I believe Mrs Cleaver was married once before she met your brother, and it may have nothing to do with this shooting, but I can't help wondering, were she and Mr Cleaver ever really married?'

CHAPTER 5

Does the earth go round the sun? Does thunder follow lightning? Is rain wet? There are questions one does not ask oneself. Gavin could have said on oath that he had never once questioned the fact that Nigel and Annabel were married.

His astonishment must have shown on his face, for Frost went on, 'Strikes you as absurd? Probably you were at their wedding yourself and know all about it.'

'Actually I wasn't,' Gavin said. 'I was abroad. I was with some friends in Vienna. I was at Oxford at the time. Of course, I knew they were probably going to get married sometime, but until I had the letter from my brother I didn't know it had happened.'

'He wrote to you, did he, telling you they'd got married?'
'Yes.'
'Where were they living then? In Tolcaster?'
'No, my brother was a lecturer in Edinburgh University

and my sister-in-law lived in London. Then the job as Deputy Director of the Cantlewell Museum in Tolcaster came up and my brother got it. That was when they got married. For some time they lived in a flat in Tolcaster, but then this house came on the market and my sister-in-law fell in love with it and snapped it up. My brother had become Director of the Museum by then and there are a number of years left before he'll have to retire, so I suppose they'd have stayed on here for life if—if things hadn't gone wrong. What my brother will do now I've no idea.'

'You don't think he'll stay on in the house alone?'

'It doesn't seem likely somehow.'

'It's worth quite a lot of money, wouldn't you say?'

'I suppose it is.'

Frost finished his coffee and put the mug down on the table beside him.

'Another thing that strikes me as kind of odd,' he said, 'is this will of Mrs Cleaver's, made a fortnight ago. It was in the drawer along with birth certificates and all that, but there's no will of Mr Cleaver's, or even a copy of one. D'you happen to know if he ever made one?'

Gavin shook his head.

'I can't remember him ever talking about it. If he did it's probably with his solicitor in London. Why don't you ask him yourself?'

'Yes, I'll do that,' Frost said. 'I just thought you might know something about it. D'you know if he's got much to leave?'

'Next to nothing, I'd guess,' Gavin answered. 'The house belonged to Annabel, I know that much, and she was a pretty wealthy woman, but I think my brother only had his salary, which wasn't vast. He'll get a pension, I believe, when he retires, and a proportion of that, a half or a third or something like that, would have gone automatically to his wife if she'd survived him, and I think that's about all.

But about this idea of yours that they might not have been married . . .'

'Yes?' Frost said.

'Have you looked at those old passports in the drawer? If they weren't married her name wouldn't have been Cleaver, would it?'

Frost gave a sardonic smile. 'Wouldn't be the first time a person made a false statement to get a passport. But that idea of mine was just an odd guess, you understand. No need to take it too seriously. The thing is, if by any chance it was right, it'll make some difference . . . But I won't bother you with that.'

'What kind of difference?' Gavin asked.

'With the Inland Revenue, to begin with.' The smile had remained on Frost's face as if the thought of making trouble for the Inland Revenue gave him a faint pleasure. 'If they were normally married, as of course I'm sure they were, there'd be no tax for your brother to pay on what he inherited from his wife. But if by any chance they weren't, there'll be quite a slice coming off it. And there's another thing—Mrs Cleaver suddenly making that will, all in a hurry, so to speak. Isn't that a bit strange? I mean, her just getting a form from the post-office, not doing it through that solicitor you mentioned in London, as if she'd suddenly become afraid of dying intestate. Or as if someone else had become afraid she might and persuaded her to get the job done, because the money wouldn't go to Nigel Beresford Cleaver, would it, if he wasn't her husband? I'm not sure where it would go. I suppose to her next-of-kin, who would have been Miss Caroline Astor, wouldn't it? There were never any children, were there?'

'No,' Gavin said. He had been growing thoughtful.

'But if Mr and Mrs Cleaver never married because she's got another husband living, then for all I know he might have got his cut, or even taken the lot. I really don't know about that. But this is all beside the point, isn't it? Your brother will be able to prove quite easily that he was married, just as everyone has always thought.'

'Yes,' Gavin said, 'I assume it will be quite easy.'

Frost got to his feet.

'Well, thanks for the coffee. And your help. And whatever I've been saying, I don't see that it affects the murder. I believe it's going to turn out quite simply that Mrs Cleaver killed Miss Astor out of jealousy, misguided or otherwise. But of course we've got to wait to hear whether or not her own death was natural. That's important. Goodbye.'

Before Gavin had had time to reach the door, the detective had let himself out into the gravelled courtyard.

Several vehicles were drawn up in front of the house opposite and there was a coming and going of uniformed men. One of the vehicles was an ambulance. Gavin closed the door, sat down in the easy chair, leant back and closed his eyes. A sudden feeling of extreme exhaustion came to him. It seemed to him as if it would be easy to escape from everything by drifting into sleep. At the same time he was struck by a sense of utter unreality. It was as if all the things that had occurred that day had never really happened, that they were all parts of a fantasy which he had constructed in a dream for some very secret purpose of his own. His walk on the downs, his acceptance of the belief that Caroline would never really care for him, his decision to leave Upthorn and drive back to Stillborough to collect his passport, to arrange with some travel agent a trip of some kind abroad, his crossing to the house to tell Nigel and Annabel that he would shortly be leaving the cottage, all faded into a dim and improbable past, a past that might have been days or weeks ago.

What had happened after that seemed even more beyond belief, a strange nightmare panorama of events of a kind with which someone like himself could not possibly have become involved. Perhaps for a little while he really did sleep. Yet when he found himself presently positively awake he was not sure whether or not he had. Time seemed to have lapsed, for looking at his watch he saw that it was just past five o'clock. Automatically he went to the television and switched it on to listen to the Saturday news.

The programme just before it had not quite finished. It was the usual instalment of sport. He first switched it off, then thought that he would stick to his habit of listening to the news and switched it on again, went and sat down in the easy chair and watched as the usual daily tale of disaster unfolded, demonstrations and riots in some country or other, destruction by football hooligans after a match, a bomb or two in Northern Ireland, an earthquake somewhere which had rendered several thousand people homeless, all neatly packaged for him to contemplate in the little cottage at Upthorn.

Was there no such thing as good news left in the world, he wondered. Was good news simply not news? Would he himself bother to watch it as regularly as he did if he were not going to be regaled by horrors? If personable young men or women were simply to appear on the screen and say, 'This is the news from the BBC. We are not at war in Europe at the moment and do not think we shall be tomorrow. The nearest war is in the Middle East. The number of people killed on the roads today has fallen by five per cent. No one that we know of has been assassinated since yesterday—' would anyone listen? No, of course not.

Then a familiar name suddenly jolted him out of his daydream.

'The novelist, Annabel Astor, died suddenly in her home today, aged sixty-one. The police are not treating her death as suspicious, but the body of her half-sister, Caroline Astor, the actress, was also found in the house in the village of Upthorn where the sisters lived, and the police are anxious to interview a man who was seen leaving the house shortly after twelve o'clock. He is described as probably in his sixties, stout, bald, wearing a dark suit and driving a grey Mercedes. Anyone who thinks they may have seen him should communicate with the Tolcaster police.'

There followed the telephone number of the police in Tolcaster.

Gavin stood up and switched the television off. He had just gone to the corner cupboard and was about to pour himself out a drink when there was a knock on the door. He went to it and opened it and Nigel came in.

While the door was open Gavin saw that most of the cars across the way had gone, the ambulance with them.

'I was just getting myself a drink,' he said. 'Want one?'

'Good idea, yes.' Nigel was carrying a black plastic bag fastened with a zip. He dumped it on a chair. His cheeks looked sunken and there were dark smears of strain under his eyes. 'Gavin, do you mind if I sleep here tonight? I've brought pyjamas and so on with me. The fact is, I can't stand being in that house alone at the moment. It was actually a bit easier while the police were still there, but they've gone now, though of course they'll be back tomorrow, and the Jays and Oliver have gone and the emptiness of the damned place is something I just can't face. It's all right if I stay with you, is it?'

'Of course, but have a drink first, then we'll think of making up a bed for you and all that,' Gavin said. 'I suppose there are sheets and so on in a cupboard somewhere.'

'Probably, though I don't much care if there aren't. Thanks.' Nigel took the glass of whisky and soda that Gavin held out to him and sat down on the window-seat. 'Gavin, d'you realize, I haven't an alibi?'

Gavin had poured out a drink for himself. He looked at his brother's drawn face in surprise.

'Have they been asking you for one?'

'Of course they have.'

'You mean they're suspicious of you?' It seemed too preposterous to Gavin to worry him much.

'Oh, they say it's just routine, but it's a singularly unpleasant thing to be asked about, especially if you can't give a satisfactory answer.'

'But weren't you at the Cantlewell?'

'Not at the time they think it happened. I'd left already.'

Gavin remembered that when Marion had tried to telephone Nigel at the museum she had been told that he had left.

'Didn't anyone see you leave?' Gavin asked.

'My secretary knows when I left the office, but I'm not sure if anyone saw me get into my car and drive off,' Nigel replied. 'Perhaps someone did.'

'But Marion Jay and Penbury and I can say when you arrived at the house, and the police will know about how long it takes to drive from Tolcaster to Upthorn, so they can work out from that where you were.'

'I wish they could.'

Gavin had returned with his drink to the easy chair. He gave Nigel a puzzled look.

'You mean you didn't drive straight home.'

'No.'

'What did you do?'

'There's a lay-by on the road between Tolcaster and Upthorn and I simply stopped there for a while. Twenty minutes or so, I should think.'

'Why did you do that?'

'I wanted to think something out, make up my mind, arrive at a decision. And I still haven't done that.'

'And you don't want to talk about it even now.'

'Not very much.'

'What have you told the police about it?'

'What I've just said to you, except that it was something to do with my work. Actually it was about leaving the Cantlewell, perhaps going abroad.'

'You really want to do that?'

'Perhaps. More now than I did.'

Gavin knew that pressing Nigel to confide in him would not result in much.

'Wasn't there any other car in the lay-by?'

'A lorry pulled in for a time and I saw the driver eating sandwiches and pouring coffee out of a Thermos,' Nigel said.

'Wasn't there the name of some company or other on the lorry?'

'There may have been. I didn't notice.'

'Anyway, if it's important the lorry can probably be traced. And there'll have been other cars going by on the road and someone in one of them may have noticed you. But I believe the police have more or less made up their minds about what happened and I don't think you need worry about yourself.'

Nigel gave Gavin a long look, then gave a slight shake of his head.

'I think I know what you mean, but they aren't really sure of it, you know,' he said.

'According to what that man Frost told me,' Gavin said, 'they believe Annabel killed Caroline out of jealousy of your relationship with her, then died herself of shock.'

'You don't believe that, do you?'

'It's a tenable theory.'

'Only Annabel wasn't jealous.'

'Frost did say the jealousy might have been misguided, by which he meant, I suppose, that in the state of mind she'd been in recently she might have been jealous even if you'd never given her cause.'

Again Nigel gave the slight shake of his head with a faint, melancholy smile.

'She wasn't jealous. But that doesn't mean she hadn't cause to be. Gavin, perhaps it'll be as well if I tell you . . .' But at that point Nigel stopped and frowned, looking as if he wished that he had not said what he had.

'You mean there was something between you and Caroline?' Gavin said, his heart for a moment thudding in his chest in an unfamiliar way.

'What I mean is, there was something for a time with someone else and Annabel knew all about it and didn't mind, in fact, up to a point she encouraged it. If you find that difficult to understand, it's because you never really knew her.'

Gavin began to feel embarrassed as he often did if people told him about sexual problems in their lives which seemed to him puzzling. His own experiences, apart from the long-standing problem of Caroline, had been fairly simple, usually leading to a mild degree of suffering which after a little while he had been able to put out of his mind. But the stability of Nigel's marriage to Annabel was something to which he would have sworn.

'Perhaps I didn't.'

That Nigel had not actually denied that there had been something between him and Caroline was something that Gavin did not think about till later.

'In a way I think it was a kind of idea she had of holding on to me,' Nigel said. 'She'd grown tired of sex herself even before her stroke and once that happened it was absolutely finished for her. But that had nothing to do with her wanting us to separate, so when she saw there was something between me and—and this other woman, she just laughed about it and more or less wished me luck. She'd just drop the odd remark to remind me that I was fairly dependent on her financially, then she'd take it back in a hurry and say she knew that didn't mean anything to me, rather as if she was afraid that I'd take it as an insult and walk out.'

'And would you have done that?'

'Probably not.'

'Her money did mean a good deal to you, then.'

'Oh yes, I always liked having it. But it wasn't why I stayed with her.'

'Why did you?' Gavin heard his own voice growing harsh as what had apparently been illusions crumbled to pieces.

'Because I loved her, damn it!' Nigel exclaimed with exasperation. 'I loved her far more than I ever cared for this woman she almost pushed in my way, and really she knew it. And that's why I say she wasn't jealous. She wasn't made that way.'

'Is the affair with the other woman still going on?' Gavin asked.

'No,' Nigel muttered in a sullen tone.

'I wouldn't ask you about it if you hadn't brought it up yourself,' Gavin said, 'but is it something the police are going to find out about?'

'I don't know.'

'But it's broken off, is it?'

'Absolutely.'

'How long ago?'

'I think we had our final quareel about a month ago. But there were so many of them I'm not really sure. Say it was a month.'

'Did Annabel know about it?'

'Oh yes. She asked me very sweetly if I was sure I wasn't making a mistake.'

'And since then she made a will.'

Nigel's eyebrows went up in a sudden look of surprise. 'That's right, of course she did. And she left everything to me. That proved she hadn't been jealous, doesn't it? She hadn't got to leave me anything.'

'If you can prove any of this.'

Nigel gave him a wary look, as if he had just started to wonder how much of it all Gavin was believing, then he stood up, went to the corner cupboard and refilled his glass.

'I don't know if I can or not,' he said gravely as he returned to the window-seat. 'I'd very much prefer not to have to. I didn't mean to talk about it even to you when I came over. With luck I can keep it quiet.'

'It would help to clear Annabel of the suspicion that she killed Caroline out of jealousy,' Gavin pointed out.

Nigel said nothing, looking thoughtful, as if he had just begun to think that perhaps it might not be specially convenient to do that. With Annabel accepted as mistakenly jealous of Caroline and herself safely dead, the whole affair would probably be cleared up with very little fuss.

'Incidentally,' Gavin said, 'why didn't Annabel make a will before? Or did she? Did you both leave wills with your solicitor?'

'No,' Nigel said. 'Neither of us made a will, I don't know why, except that it was always something we meant to do but never got around to doing. I didn't bother about my own, because I'd virtually nothing to leave. And Annabel was one of the people who shrink from making a will, as if doing it brings death that much closer. I rather think it was Caroline who persuaded her to do it. I remember Annabel talking to me about it soon after Caroline offered to stay on to look after her, and if she talked about it to Caroline too that may have made Caroline pretty determined to get Annabel to put down something in writing. I'm not saying it was why Caroline came to stay, mind. That was sheer kindness.'

'She'd no other reason for coming?'

'No. Why?'

'Just that I've had a slightly disturbing talk with Marion Jay, who seems to be sure she had some more interesed reason for coming. By the way, who is James Boyce?'

'Jim Boyce? He's our gardener. He comes out from Up-thorn once a week and keeps things more or less in order.'

'It's only that he and Mrs Nevin witnessed the will. I realize you couldn't have done that as you were a benefici-ary, but do you know that Frost thinks there's something a bit peculiar about the way the will is worded?'

'I think he's a bit surprised that it's just on a form from the post-office, instead of something drawn up with all the legal pomp we'd have got from a solicitor, but that's all he's said about it to me.'

Gavin was tempted to leave it at that. In fact, he thought that at that point he might suggest that they should go up-stairs to make up Nigel's bed for him and that after that they might discuss what they should do about some kind of evening meal. There were some eggs in the refrigerator, Gavin remembered. He might make scrambled eggs. Or perhaps they should just stick to bread and cheese and more whisky.

But something would not let him drop the subject of the will yet. Mostly curiosity, perhaps, though there was a dis-turbing tinge of fear in it that drove him on.

'As Frost put it to me,' he said, 'he finds it strange that Annabel doesn't refer to you in the will as her husband, but only by your name. It's led him to wonder if in fact you and she were actually married.'

There was a moment of silence, then a curious smile ap-peared on Nigel's face.

'Clever devil,' he observed.

'You mean it's true?'

Nigel nodded, the smile broadening.

'Don't look so shocked, Gavin,' he said. 'We'd excellent reasons.'

'I'm only startled,' Gavin said lamely.

'Naturally.' Nigel did not seem at all put out. 'You know,

of course, that Annabel's first marriage didn't last long and
Halliday faded completely out of her life. Then some years
later they suddenly met by chance and he told her then
he'd married again. Only unfortunately they'd never
bothered with the formality of a divorce, so he'd committed bigamy. Annabel offered to give him a divorce then so
that he could get properly married, but he was horrified at
the idea and implored her to do nothing about it. His wife
knew nothing about his first marriage and if she had, and
even if he and Annabel had been divorced, she'd never have
married him, being a very strict Catholic. So he'd taken the
risk of bigamy and if Annabel had gone ahead with a divorce
it would not only have shattered this second marriage of his,
but got him in trouble with the law. So being the good-
natured soul she was, she let him get away with it, but later
on, of course, it meant that she and I couldn't get married as
we didn't feel like risking bigamy ourselves. So we just told
people we were married and nobody questioned it. They
don't, you know, unless some legal difficulties arise where
marriage has to be proved. I mean, they don't trot along to
Somerset House to check that you really signed up properly,
they just accept what you say and some of them even send
you wedding presents. You sent us a very nice Norwegian de-
canter and set of wine-glasses, with apologies because it was
arriving a bit late for the actual marriage.'

'But the passports,' Gavin said. 'Her name must really
have been Halliday, but in your old passports it's Cleaver.'

'Ever heard of deed-poll?'

'Yes, I've heard of people changing their names by
deed-poll, but I don't know much about it.'

'Well, it's what she did. When we were sure that we were
really going to go on living together and that what we'd got
was really a marriage, we decided it would be convenient
if we had the same name, so we did it legally and that came
in useful when we started to do a good deal of travelling,

staying in hotels and so on. Things weren't quite as permissive as they are now, or if they really were we preferred to avoid the possible embarrassments of having different names. It was playing safe too when I took the job in Tolcaster and we settled there. While I was still working in Edinburgh and she was in London and we were only having weekends together it didn't signify, but once we moved down here together we thought it would be best to get the job done. Income Tax has been our only problem. I'm assessed as a married man, so I believe we may have cheated the government out of a few thousands.'

'When this all comes out, as I suppose it will now, it'll make some difference to your inheritance, as Frost pointed out to me,' Gavin said.

'A pity, but there'll still be plenty left,' Nigel replied. 'In any case, none of this makes any difference to what happened to Caroline, does it?'

'Not that I can see.' Gavin stood up. 'But if there hadn't been a murder, with the police looking into things, you might have got away with paying no tax, mightn't you?'

'It's possible.'

'Would you have tried it on?'

'Probably.' Nigel gave an abrupt laugh. 'Now suppose we go and make up that bed of yours.'

They went up the narrow stairs together, found sheets and blankets in a cupboard in the second bedroom, made up the bed there, then went downstairs again and Gavin made toast and scrambled some eggs in the kitchen while Nigel sat by himself in the living-room, gradually consuming another whisky.

Gavin was in a deeply confused state of mind. It seemed to him that he had never known his brother. He had always assumed that there was a good deal of understanding between them, yet what Nigel had told him almost casually about himself indicated that there had been next to none.

On the whole Gavin felt that he should blame himself for this. He had been too naïve, too lacking in perception to have been taken into his brother's confidence.

It hurt to discover that he had never been trusted with the truth. He wondered if anyone else had been, Caroline for instance. Not that he could see how her possible knowledge of it could have affected her grisly end and he had no reason to think that she had known any more than he had. And after all, what he had not known was not in itself so very important. However, it was painful to learn what a fool he had been. For a time, as he was beating the eggs before scrambling them, he found himself sharply resenting Nigel's presence in the cottage and wondering too how much of what he had just been told was the truth. If Nigel could lie to him for twenty years, why should he suddenly stop doing so now?

Why should Gavin believe that there had been nothing between Nigel and Caroline, that there had ever been an affair between him and some unnamed woman, that this had ended and that Annabel had never suffered from jealousy? And suppose there had been such an affair, who had the woman been? Leslie Jay, possibly. She was on the spot and perhaps available. True, her mother had said that she was probably to be married soon to young Dr Penbury, but in the mood that Gavin was in he was disinclined to believe in the truthfulness of anybody, even someone as apparently open and honest as Marion Jay. And even if she was honest, she might be deceived, might she not? She was afraid that her husband was deceiving her. But Leslie might not be the only woman in Nigel's life. He had a secretary and no doubt many other female acquaintances. Gavin scowled at the eggs as they thickened in the saucepan and when presently he dished them up, he ate his plateful silently, wondering if what was really the matter with him was a simple attack of envy because all their lives Nigel had always been the more sexually successful of the two of them, had generally seemed to get what he wanted and found the organizing of his life a relatively simple matter.

They had finished their supper and were washing it up before Nigel suddenly said, 'When you went over to the house this morning, Gavin, there was some reason you did, wasn't there? You said something about it.'

'Nothing important,' Gavin answered.

'You were just dropping in, were you?'

'That's all.'

'I've a feeling, I'm not sure why, that there was something more to it.'

Gavin turned off the tap under which he had been rinsing the plates that they had used.

'Really, there was a reason, but it doesn't amount to anything now,' he said. 'I was just going to tell you that I'd changed my mind about staying on here for the rest of the summer and was going to try to fix up a trip abroad. I thought I'd stay on for the weekend, then set off for home.'

'Bored already, were you?'

'It wasn't boredom. It was meeting Caroline again. I'd been wanting to do that for a long time to find out what if anything we meant to one another, but before I'd got as far as sorting out my own feelings I realized she hadn't any use for me. And I suppose I was a bit scared because I was afraid that was going to mean more than I'd thought it would. And then, of all things, while I was wondering what to do, Helena telephoned and threatened to come and stay with me here.'

'Oh God!'

'That's what I felt.'

'Isn't she coming?'

'I did my best to put her off, but you know it isn't always easy to cope with her. So I thought the simplest thing for me to do would be to make for home and that's what I went over to tell you this morning. But the way things are, of course I can't simply leave. Now there's something you can tell me, Nigel.'

Nigel hung the tea-towel he had been using over the back of a chair.

'I thought I'd told you just about everything,' he said as he strolled back to the living-room.

He dropped into the easy chair, leaving the window-seat to Gavin.

'It's only that when you suggested I should come and stay here,' Gavin said, his mind still full of distrust of his brother, 'you seemed unusually eager that I should. It wasn't altogether like you. I know we've seen very little of each other for a fair time, but I remember it struck me as slightly odd. Had you in fact any special reason for wanting me to come?'

'Only that it seemed a good idea that for once we should see something of each other. I think the idea was Annabel's. I don't think there was anything special about it. What could there be?'

It might have been merely because of his new distrust of Nigel, but Gavin could not avoid a feeling that this was not the truth.

'I've no idea,' he said. 'There really wasn't anything?'

Nigel yawned. 'If you knew how tired I am . . . Not that it's exactly tiredness, I suppose. It's more a feeling of everything having come to an end. One doesn't live through days like this very often. I can't even begin to think. I think I'll go to bed.'

Again Gavin noticed that his question had not been answered. 'All right,' he said.

'Not that I'm likely to sleep, but I think I'll go.'

'Have another drink first. It may help.'

'No thanks. Good night.'

'Good night.'

Nigel stood up and walked, heavy-footed, to the bottom of the stairs. He paused there, as if he had thought of something more that he wanted to say, but then he slowly climbed the stairs. Gavin heard him walking about in the room overhead, but then there was silence.

It was not long before Gavin followed him up to his own room, expecting that he would not be able to sleep, but there seemed to be nothing to do downstairs but to go on drinking and brooding and he had already had as much whisky as he wanted. He wondered about next day. How was it to be spent? Until the police told him that he could leave he would have to stay, even though he would be of no particular use to anybody. For a little while he lay in bed awake, his thoughts straying over what Nigel had told him and also what he had not told him. For instance, the identity of the woman with whom he had claimed to have had a love-affair. Was it Leslie Jay? Or could it conceivably have been Leslie's mother, Marion?

Of the two of them, Gavin thought, he himself would sooner have had an affair with the mother than with the daughter. That was something to think about. Was it a possibility, or was he losing himself in far from convincing fantasies? At some point, before he had sorted this out, he drifted into sleep and slept heavily and dreamlessly until the sound of someone moving about in the kitchen below woke him.

The time was eight o'clock and the sound that had wakened him had been made by Nigel getting the breakfast. The scent of freshly made coffee rose to him. He got up, put on his dressing-gown and went downstairs.

'I've been thinking,' Nigel greeted him. He was dressed and had made coffee and toast and was seated at the small table in the kitchen. 'It's going to be best if I go back to the house, isn't it? That's where the police are likely to come looking for me.'

'Just as you like,' Gavin said.

'You could move over too, if you felt like it.'

'There's no need for me to move my things over, is there? I can still sleep here. But I can spend the day with you, if that's what you want. What sort of night did you have?'

'Pretty bad. I think I'll ask Desmond to give me some sleeping-pills.'

'I wonder how his cricket went yesterday.'

'Cricket, oh my God, yes! I'd forgotten about that. I suppose all the time the police were here he was happily playing cricket.'

'You think he went straight from his surgery, or wherever he was, to the cricket field, do you?'

'I suppose he had lunch somewhere.'

'But you don't know where?'

'Gavin, what are you thinking about?'

'I'm not quite sure.'

'Anyway, Marion must have told him all about things when he got home. In a way I'm surprised he hasn't been round.'

'Will he have anything to do with the post-mortem?'

'I doubt it. The police have their own forensic man in Tolcaster. But Desmond may have gone to find out what he could. That probably explains why we haven't heard from him. I wonder when we're going to hear the results ourselves.'

'Fairly soon, I should think. There can't be anything particularly complicated about them.'

In fact, there was not. Gavin heard the results from Detective-Inspector Frost at about ten o'clock that morning. Nigel had gone by then and Gavin had cleared away the breakfast things, had had a shower and dressed and been at the window of the living-room, wondering if he should go over to the house when he saw a police car draw up in front of it. It made him decide to wait for a time, because if the police wanted to talk to him they were liable to want to do it privately and they could do that as easily in the cottage as across the way. It was about half an hour later that Frost, attended by Detective-Constable Crewe, arrived at the cottage.

As Gavin let them in Frost said, 'Fine morning, but I don't think it's going to last. Wind's in the wrong direction. We'll have rain by the afternoon.'

The tone of his voice was genial, but there was what struck Gavin as a careful expressionlessness in the man's wide-spaced, dark eyes which filled him with a sense of caution. Gavin himself had had no thoughts yet about the weather that morning. He mumbled a greeting, invited Frost to take the easy-chair and Crewe the window-seat, then chose one of the wooden chairs in the room for himself.

'There are one or two things I want to ask you, if you don't mind,' Frost said. 'Matter of some loose ends, that's all. Just routine. You don't have to answer if you don't want to.'

For some reason that frightened Gavin. Wasn't it the sort of thing they said to you if you were under suspicion of something? But why should that worry him? As Frost said, just routine. He was probably about to ask Gavin for his alibi and the fact that he did not happen to have one, unless perhaps the stranger with the Mercedes could give him one, if he could be traced, was not a reason why for an instant he should feel the unusual pounding of his heart which he had noticed once the day before.

'Anything I can do to help,' he said.

'Good,' Frost replied. 'But first there are one or two things I'd better tell you. You'll find them interesting. First, there's absolutely no doubt that Mrs Cleaver died a natural death. Cerebral haemorrhage. A stroke, that's to say. Whether or not it was brought on by shock or was going to happen anyway may be one of the things we'll never know.

And Miss Astor died from a bullet wound in the brain, shot at close range from the gun that was lying on the floor beside her sister. Of that there's no possible doubt. There's one rather surprising fact, however. There are no fingerprints on that gun. Not Mrs Cleaver's, or Miss Astor's, or anyone else's. It had been wiped clean before being left beside Mrs Cleaver.'

CHAPTER 6

Gavin gave himself a moment to try to think out what that meant.

'So there was someone else in the house who did the actual shooting of Miss Astor,' he said.

'That's how it looks, but it isn't absolutely certain,' Frost replied.

'Why not?' Gavin asked. 'I'd have said it was obvious.'

'It's just that Mrs Cleaver might have wiped the gun clean before doing the shooting. Otherwise you'll agree, you'd expect her prints to be on it, and probably Mr Cleaver's too, because I believe he picked the gun up the previous evening after Mrs Cleaver had played her little game with it. But as there aren't any prints at all there, it seems to mean either that someone else handled the gun, wiping it clean afterwards before dropping it beside Mrs Cleaver, or else that she wiped it clean herself before killing her sister and still had it wrapped in something when she collapsed. She could have been on her way to hide it somewhere in the garden when she fell down.'

Gavin shook his head. 'No, that isn't in character.'

'Too deliberate, you think? Too carefully planned?'

'Much. I think she was an impulsive, emotional woman. I can just imagine that in some moment of mad rage she decided to kill her sister, but I can't imagine her carefully thinking out beforehand that she mustn't risk leaving her fingerprints on the gun. I don't think she was at all cunning.'

'If you'd seen what I have of people acting out of character when it comes to crime!' Frost said. 'The things they'll do which their loved ones who've known them all their lives, and been seeing them day after day, say are simply out of the question!'

'Well, supposing Mrs Cleaver did do what you suggest,' Gavin said, 'what happened to the cloth, or the handkerchief, or the gloves, or even the yellow duster in which she used to keep the gun wrapped? Did you find anything of the sort near her body?'

'No, and that of course supports your belief that she didn't shoot her sister and that some third person was in the house for a little while with the two women, and he's the one we've got to find.'

'That man I saw come running out of the house and taking off in his Mercedes!'

'Only how did he know where Mrs Cleaver kept her gun?'

Again Gavin took a moment to think before he answered. Then he said hesitantly, 'I suppose you mean it must have been one of us who was at dinner with the Cleavers on Friday evening. We all saw my brother put the gun away in the drawer of the bureau. But that isn't absolutely certain, is it?'

'No,' Frost agreed. 'One of the things that could have happened is that either Mrs Cleaver or Miss Astor took the gun out of the drawer and then left it somewhere where that man you saw might have seen it and decided to use it. That would make the murder unpremeditated, of course. Or Miss Astor may have shot herself, or Mrs Cleaver shot her, but in any case Mrs Cleaver carried the gun into the drawing-room and there came face to face with this stranger you've told us about, who thought she was pointing it at him and who grabbed it from her and after perhaps a bit of a struggle, in the middle of which she collapsed and died, he wiped the gun clean and left it by her body before making off as fast as he could.'

'Were there any marks of violence on Mrs Cleaver's body?' Gavin asked.

'No.'

'No bruises, no scratches, no traces of blood?'

'Not one. But there's something it may be important to remember and that is that this third person in the house may not have been the stranger you saw. He may have been a fourth person who walked in on the scene after everything had happened and very naturally got away as fast as possible. So we've got to check on the movements of a fair number of people. Most of it's pure routine, but we've got to go through with it.'

'I thought we'd get around to that sooner or later,' Gavin said. 'You want my alibi.'

'Well, it would help if we could anyway cross you off our list,' Frost replied.

'Only I'm afraid you can't.'

Frost put a hand up to his heavy jaw and rubbed it thoughtfully. A look that might have been one of impatience appeared in his hitherto expressionless eyes.

'There's no one who can say where you were between, say, eleven and twelve o'clock?' he said. 'You see, both women had been dead only a very short time when we arrived on the scene. Not much more than half an hour, we believe. So we can pinpoint the time of their deaths fairly exactly.'

'I think I told you yesterday I went for a walk on the downs in the morning,' Gavin said. 'I'm not sure what time it was that I got back. About a quarter or half past eleven,

I think. Then soon after I got in Miss Jay called to invite me to drinks at the Jays' house this morning. She stayed only ten minutes or so, I think, then only a little while after she left I had a telephone call from a sister of mine who lives in London. We chatted for a few minutes and it was after that that I went across to the house to speak to my brother and as I was starting out saw the man I've described to you come rushing out of the house. I tried knocking on the front door after he'd gone, but got no answer, so I went round to the terrace and walked in at the door of the drawing-room, and—well, I think that was about twelve o'clock. So you see, except for the short time when Miss Jay was with me, there's no one who can say where I was at the relevant time, except possibly that man. Just possibly he could tell you I was standing in the doorway here when he came out of the house. But I doubt if he was in a condition to notice anything at that time.'

'Now wait a moment,' Frost said. 'You had a telephone call, you say, from your sister.'

'Yes.'

'Can you tell me just what time she called you?'

'Exactly, no.'

'But perhaps she could.'

Gavin thought of the vague and dreamy world in which Helena lived and shook his head.

'I think it's most unlikely.'

'She can say she spoke to you, however. She had your number.'

'No, she told me she had some difficulty in getting it. She began by ringing me up at Stillborough, couldn't get an answer, so got hold of my landlord and he told her that I'd gone to stay with my brother. So she rang up his number and got Miss Astor and she gave him my number here, and it was then she rang me up here—'

'Now wait a moment!' Frost interrupted again. 'She rang

up your brother's number and spoke to Miss Astor?'

'So she said.'

'And straight away, after doing that, she rang you up?'

'I suppose so. She didn't actually say she'd done it straight away.'

'But it's your opinion that it's what she did?'

'I think so.'

'Then don't you see what that means? Miss Astor was alive to answer the telephone when your sister called her. But when you went over to the house only a few minutes later, she was dead. So that tells us pretty exactly when she died.'

'And the fact that the telephone here was ringing at the time explains why I didn't hear the shot.'

'That's right. Yes, that's right.' A gleam of enthusiasm appeared in Frost's eyes. He was becoming, little by little, more human. 'You must give me your sister's address and telephone number, of course. But now tell me something that's puzzling me. Here I am, sitting in this chair, and even though Crewe's sitting on the window-seat I can see past him into that courtyard. So why didn't you see the Mercedes arrive there? I gather you didn't.'

'No,' Gavin said. 'But if it was when Miss Jay was here, she was sitting in that chair and I was sitting on the window-seat with my back to the window. I wouldn't have seen anything.'

'But perhaps she did.'

'If she did, it doesn't seem to have interested her. She's said nothing about it.'

'It's something we can ask her about, all the same. Well now, that address of your sister's, if you don't mind.'

Gavin gave it to him and Crewe made a note of it.

'And you're staying on here for the present, I take it,' Frost said.

'Yes,' Gavin replied.

'Good. And thank you for your help.'

The two detectives departed.

It was an immense relief to Gavin when they left, even more than he had been expecting. He did not realize until they had gone how much fear he had been repressing while they were there. But simply to be alone now made him feel so suddenly able to relax that it seemed absurd that he should have felt that he was in the least danger. But at the back of his mind there had lurked the thought that if certain things were to be said to the police they might take him to be the person with the best motive for murdering Caroline. Whether anyone had said those things to them or was likely to say them he did not know. Probably not, he thought. He had just been suffering from a fit of totally irrational panic. But to be alone in the small room now felt very refreshing and pleasant. He began to feel quite fond of it.

It was Mrs Nevin who presently intruded on him.

She arrived on her bicycle, propped it on the wall beside the door and knocked. When Gavin opened the door, she stood hesitantly on the threshold, looking unsure of herself. She was in what he supposed was her Sunday wear, not the trousers in which she worked but a smart scarlet suit with some white frills at her throat and with her fair curls loose on her shoulders.

'If I'm not intruding . . .' she said diffidently and waited for him to assure her she was not.

He did so at once. 'Of course you aren't, Mrs Nevin—Beatrice. It's very good of you to come. You've heard of what happened here, I suppose.'

'Oh yes, it's all round the village.' She stepped into the room. 'It's not only that it was on television, and what a thing that was to see all of a sudden, but Bob Crewe's grandmother lives in Upthorn and he was in to see her yesterday evening. So I thought, even if it isn't one of my days for going there, I'll go up and see if there's anything I can do to help. You've only to say. Both the poor ladies at once! You and Mr Cleaver must be in a terrible state, not knowing what to do about anything. I can just cook you a little lunch if you like and leave you something for your supper. I did think perhaps you'd be going to the Upthorn Inn. They do a very nice lunch and on any other day of the week you could get fish and chips to take away, which might suit you better, but they don't do that on a Sunday. And then I thought anyway you wouldn't care to go where everyone will be looking at you and talking about the things that happened here and so that's why I came.'

'That's truly very kind of you,' Gavin said. 'You're quite right, I don't suppose we'll be going to the Upthorn Inn, but I'm sure we can manage to cook something for ourselves. But do sit down and have a drink. What would you like, some sherry, or would you sooner have a cup of coffee?'

'Some sherry would be very nice, though it seems kind of early for it,' she said as she perched herself on the edge of the window-seat. 'You're sure I couldn't cook you up some pork chops with some peas and potatoes? I know there are some pork chops in the freezer in the other house and there's some ice-cream too. It really wouldn't be any trouble.'

Gavin had gone to the corner cupboard and was pouring out sherry for them both.

'The fact is, I don't feel very hungry,' he said as he brought a glass to Mrs Nevin. 'And I don't expect my brother does either. I should think we'll make do with some bread and cheese, though I'm very grateful for your offer. Beatrice, may I ask you something?'

He sat down in the easy chair, feeling a little surprised at the thought that had just come to him.

'Of course,' she said, 'though I don't suppose there's anything much I can tell you. I've never had such a shock in my life as when I saw that on television. I've known for some time Mrs Cleaver wasn't well and might be taken any time, but that someone should come into the house and batter Miss Astor to death, that man in the grey car, is more than I'd ever have believed.'

'She wasn't actually battered to death,' Gavin said, 'she was shot, and it isn't at all certain that it was the man in the grey car who did it, even if it seems probable. But as things stand at the moment, the police only want to question him.'

'Is that right?' Mrs Nevin said, sipping her sherry. 'I thought it was him for certain. It just shows you can't believe everything you're told. I forget just who it was—oh, I know, it was Mrs Secombe, old Mrs Crewe's next-door neighbour—who told me about the way the murder happened and the blood and all. But she must have got things wrong. Now what was it you wanted to ask me?'

'I just wanted to ask if you remember witnessing a will that Mrs Cleaver signed about a fortnight ago,' Gavin said.

She looked puzzled. 'A will? No, I don't remember witnessing any will.'

'You and James Boyce. I believe he's the gardener here. Didn't you and James Boyce witness Mrs Cleaver's signature on her will?'

'Oh, that,' she said. 'Yes, Jim Boyce and I witnessed her signature the same as I often did, but it wasn't on any will, not that I understood.'

'But your signature's there on her will,' Gavin said. 'Didn't you know it was her will she was signing?'

She frowned thoughtfully. 'I can't say I did. You're sure that's what it was—her will?'

He nodded.

'Of course, I did think it was unusual, her wanting Jim to sign,' she went on. 'Usually it's only me, but Miss Astor told me this time it had to be two people.'

'What was it you usually signed for her?' Gavin asked.

'The contracts on her books in America,' she answered. 'Her English publishers didn't bother her about a witness, so I understand, but the one in America always wanted her to get someone to watch her sign. So I did it for her, oh, any number of times. And that's what I thought I was signing a couple of weeks ago. But it was a will, you say. I'm sure she said it was a contract.'

'You didn't read it to see what you were signing?'

'Oh dear me, no. I hadn't got my glasses with me, for one thing. I can see well enough to write my own name without them, and I saw her write hers, but I couldn't have read it, even if I thought I should, which never struck me. It was just another form to me, typewritten, you know, not hand-written, and not something it was my business to read. And Jim Boyce just signed his name under mine and that was that.'

'And neither Mrs Cleaver nor Miss Astor told you it was a will you were signing?'

She shook her head.

'You're sure?'

'Oh yes, a will, I'd have remembered that. I mean, signing a will, that's a serious thing. No, I'm sure one or other of them said it was a contract. I think it was Miss Astor. Mrs Cleaver was always signing contracts. You know she wrote ever so many books. Even after she was taken ill she wrote two, that's to say, I think she dictated them on to tape or something, because the poor thing couldn't use her typewriter with her hands not quite what they should be. I think Mr Cleaver, or perhaps it was Miss Astor, typed them out for her in the evenings, only I think it was Mr Cleaver, because I remember Miss Astor saying once she could only type with two fingers. I used to find heaps of typewritten sheets on the desk by her typewriter when I went in to clean. He was ever so good to her. It isn't every

man who'd have done a thing like that when he got home
tired from his own work.'

'And Miss Astor was in the room when you witnessed
what you thought was a contract?' Gavin asked.

'Yes.'

'Was my brother there too?'

She shook her head once more. 'No, he was away at his
work.' She wrinkled her forehead with a look of anxiety.
'Have I done something wrong, Mr Cleaver?'

'No, no, not in the least,' he said. 'It's just that it's rather
strange that my sister-in-law made her will as she did instead of getting it done by the family solicitor. I couldn't
help feeling a little puzzled about it, but that's all.'

Only it was not quite all. It was not until after Mrs Nevin
had gone that Gavin succeeded in identifying what it was
that she had said that had puzzled him. It was simply those
heaps of typescript that she used to find beside Annabel's
typewriter when she came to clean in the mornings. It had
sounded very noble of Nigel, or perhaps it was Caroline, to
do Annabel's typing for her, but if the truth was that she
had dictated those last two books of hers on to tapes, why
had the tapes not simply been sent to a professional typist?
That surely would have been the obvious thing to do with
them. It was a little strange that this apparently had not
been done.

Gavin remembered then something else that at the time
had not struck him as strange, though now it began to
worry him. It was Annabel's anxious inquiry when he had
been with her on the terrace, waiting for Caroline to bring
them tea, as to what other people had said to him about
her last books. Had they said anything about them? Had
they said they were worse than usual, or just possibly better? She had claimed to think herself that they were lousy,
that had been her word for them, and it had all seemed
natural enough to Gavin as the anxiety of a sick woman

that her work was deteriorating. But now he found the memory of it curiously disturbing.

He began to wonder if it was possible that Annabel had not written these books since her stroke, but had had them, perhaps for years, in a drawer, either because they had been rejected at some time in the past and eventually had been published only because all her work had become so popular, or because she had written more than her publisher could manage to cope with and was waiting to bring them to light on some occasion when there was a longer gap than usual between her books. Not that that explained the heap of typescript that Mrs Nevin had seen, because even if the old manuscript had needed retyping, that could have been done by a professional, just as the tapes could have been. But was any of this important?

The only possible importance in it that Gavin could see was that if Annabel's two new books had not been written since her stroke it might indicate that her condition had not improved as much as was generally thought. The fact that she had written the two books seemed to have been accepted as a sign that she had gone a long way towards complete mental recovery, even if she remained slightly disabled physically. But if she had not written them then, yet had insisted on their being published even though she could not have been in any need of money, might it not mean that she had still been tragically unbalanced at the time of her death? In other words, might it not mean that she could have been capable of killing her sister out of repressed jealousy, even if Nigel was certain that this could not be the case? Might she not have been a murderess?

But what about the absence of fingerprints on the gun?

'I've got to stop this,' Gavin heard himself say aloud, 'or I'll be starting to think I killed Caroline myself.'

The best thing to do, he thought, would be to go over to see Nigel and discuss the matter of the books with him, because he must know the truth about them. The police car had gone and Nigel was presumably alone. Gavin opened the door and stepped out into the courtyard. As he did so a taxi turned in at the gate, seemed about to stop at the door of the house opposite, then drove on along the gravelled drive and came to a stop at the cottage.

'Oh God, it's Helena after all!' Gavin thought with a feeling of desperation. He had believed that he had managed to put her off, yet here she was.

Only he was wrong. It was not Helena who descended from the taxi, but his elder sister, Barbara.

It was several years since Gavin had seen her last, but she had changed very little in the time. She was forty-five now, tall, thin but muscular, and was dressed as she nearly always had been in shabby grey trousers and a loose, rather badly hand-knitted jersey. Her hair, which had gone grey at an early age, was cropped shorter than Gavin's. She had a long, pointed face with a long, thin nose, a narrow mouth and singularly bright and beautiful blue eyes. Gavin remembered that when they had all been young he had admired her greatly. Her thinness had been supple and athletic and had not yet become bony, her features were delicately formed and her complexion had been shining. She had married early and to the best of his knowledge the marriage had been happy, yet it seemed to have precipitated a change in her, turning her into a brusque, domineering woman, a change that had only deepened with the years, particularly since her husband had died ten years ago.

She got out of the taxi backwards, hauling her luggage after her. Gavin went to help her with it and she promptly thrust into his arms a large basket containing, as far as he could see, a cabbage, some carrots, a lettuce or two, some tomatoes, some plums, and some eggs.

'I meant to go straight to the house to see Nigel,' she

greeted him in her deep, rather gruff voice, 'then I saw you standing here so I thought I'd come round and ask you how things are over there. You don't look very well, Gavin. Are you taking proper care of yourself?'

They did not kiss. Gavin could not remember that they had ever kissed one another.

'I'm all right,' he said. 'How are you?'

'Oh, you know me,' she answered. She was paying the taxi-driver. 'I manage to keep going somehow, though my digestion's as troublesome as ever. It's all that junk food we were given to eat as children. But one mustn't give in. How's Nigel?'

'You know what's happened here, do you?' Gavin asked.

'Why else do you think I'm here?' The taxi drove off. 'I saw about it on television and thought: If Nigel's got himself into trouble I'd better stand by him, even if it doesn't occur to him to say thank you. I didn't know about you being here. I thought he was probably alone. And I brought those things in the basket as a goodwill gesture, all good stuff, grown naturally, no beastly fertilizers. Where are you staying? Here in the cottage or over in the house?'

'Here,' Gavin said.

'Well, shall I stay here with you or over the way with Nigel? I suppose the place is full of policemen. Perhaps they won't want someone extra around.'

'We'd better discuss that with Nigel, I think. He stayed here himself last night and I don't know if he means to come back or stay there. But come in here now and have some tea or coffee or something.' He remembered that she never touched alcohol. 'You must be tired after the journey. How did you come, by train?'

'Do you imagine I came on wings?' As usual, she was sarcastic.

'No, it was a silly question. I was just thinking perhaps you'd driven, but I was forgetting the taxi.' He picked up her suitcase and carried it and the basket of garden produce into the cottage. 'Tea or coffee?'

'Tea, thank you, if you can manage that.' She dropped into the easy chair. She really did look tired. 'I was up at dawn this morning, caught the early train to Paddington, got a taxi to Waterloo, then came on here. What hell London is! Disgusting smells, dirt everywhere and people—far too many people!'

'It certainly isn't what it used to be, but wouldn't it be difficult to exterminate the people?'

'It'd do a lot of good. I don't know how Helena can live there. Have you heard anything of her lately?'

'As a matter of fact, we were talking on the telephone yesterday.'

'You're honoured. She doesn't speak to me. Now tell me about Nigel and Annabel and all. They didn't really say much on television and I left too early to get a newspaper.'

'Just wait till I've got the tea, then I'll tell you everything.'

Gavin went out to the kitchen, filled the kettle and started to make the tea.

Barbara's comment when he brought the tray into the living-room had nothing to do with the murder.

'Tea-bags!' she said.

'I'm afraid so, yes,' Gavin said. 'They're what I found here in the cottage and they do make things easier.'

'They're not natural,' she said. All the same, she seemed glad of the tea. 'Now go ahead and tell me everything.'

He told her very nearly everything. He told her of the dinner-party on Friday evening and of Annabel's strange antics then with the gun. He told her of Leslie's visit the next morning. He told her of his discovery of the bodies of the two women, of the gun found beside Annabel and that it had no fingerprints on it. He told her of the stranger whom he had seen leaving the house.

He even told her, though he hesitated before doing it, that Nigel and Annabel had never been married. He was not quite sure if it was right to tell her this, but thought that after all the police must know about it and Nigel himself had dropped all attempt to keep it secret. Almost the only thing that he left out was Nigel's confession that he had been involved in an affair with another woman until only a month ago. He mentioned the books that Annabel had written recently, but not his perplexities about them, and the will, witnessed by Mrs Nevin and James Boyce. Barbara was an attentive listener who interrupted only with an occasional question when she found something that he had said not quite clear. There was a slight frown on her long, rather severe face all the time she sat there, her gaze steadily and almost unblinkingly on his. When he became silent and it was clear that he had no more to tell her, she nodded her head as if she were accepting the fact that her original question to him had been adequately answered and that she gave him tolerably good marks for it.

'And you didn't murder Caroline yourself, I suppose,' she said.

'No, I did not,' Gavin answered.

'It's only that if you did you would be quite safe, telling me so. I should respect your confidence.'

'Blood being thicker than water.'

'Exactly. Not that that's a thing I've always felt sure about in our family. But in a time of trial you learn a lot about yourself. You were in love with her, weren't you?'

'One doesn't automatically murder all the women one's been in love with.'

'I didn't intend to imply that you did. But weren't you in love with her and didn't she let you down?'

He thought that the easiest way to put an end to this line of questioning was to admit it. 'In a way, yes,' he said.

'And the police are aware of the fact?'

'I haven't told them so myself. I don't know what Nigel's told them.'

'If he thought they were suspicious of him, he'd certainly have told them. You can't trust Nigel an inch. He'll pose and equivocate and lie as much as happens to be convenient for him. I don't believe you ever understood that about him. There was such a difference in age between you, he was always just the brilliant older brother to you. But I always knew there was something peculiar about that marriage. Not just the difference in age. I know that needn't be of any importance. But it was all out of character, you know, the quiet affair at the registry office with none of us even being sure who the witnesses were. They ought to have had a really ostentatious sort of wedding with lots of guests and champagne and all and perhaps even the press. That's what Annabel would have loved. I suppose you've had the press here about her murder—I mean, her death, her oh, so natural death. Do you honestly think it was natural, Gavin?'

'I told you, the medicals and the police are quite certain about it,' he answered.

'I wonder if they're really as certain as all that, or if it just suits them to say so. You say they asked for your alibi.'

He was becoming very irritated with her. 'That was for Caroline's murder or suicide. They'll probably ask you for yours before they're done.'

'And quite right of them too,' she said. 'Luckily I'll be able to supply one without much difficulty. But about Nigel, Gavin, isn't he the most obvious suspect?'

'You think he shot Caroline?'

'It seems to me very probable.'

'Why?'

'Suppose he was in love with her and she kicked him in the teeth. Perhaps she even told him she had another lover. He's vain enough for anything, you know. That may be another of the things about him you've never understood.'

He nearly told her then what Nigel had told him of his affair with another woman, but decided to continue to suppress it. As he did so, however, he remembered his own bitter feeling the evening before because of his failure to understand his brother. To what extent, he found himself wondering now, had he been completely deceived by him?

'And there's always the possibility that Caroline was blackmailing him,' Barbara went on.

He stared at her blankly. 'Blackmailing him? For God's sake, what about? What a foul mind you've got, Barbara!'

'But doesn't it stare one in the face?' she said calmly. 'Living with them, she almost certainly knew that marriage was a phoney. And neither of them would have liked it if that had come out. Haven't you ever come across any of the interviews with Annabel in the women's magazines? Not that I suppose you read them, nor do I normally unless I'm stuck in the waiting-room in our doctor's surgery, and that isn't often, because all he does is give me pills and they never do me any good. I've tried some once or twice and they just gave me the most fearful stomach upsets, so I flushed them down the lavatory, and I told him so, so he just gave me some more which were even worse . . . But what was I saying? Oh yes, Annabel and her happy marriage that she loved to tell the reporters all about, with pictures of her lovely home and all. And if the truth had come out, I don't suppose it would have done Nigel any good in his job, even if nowadays it wouldn't have done him much harm. But they'd both have looked such fools, wouldn't they? And then there's the possibility that he was having affairs with other women—after all, it must be quite difficult not to when you're as good-looking as he is—and Caroline might have known about them and threatened to tell Annabel. Oh, I don't think one can rule blackmail out as a possible motive. Now let's go over and talk to Nigel.

We've got to settle where I'm going to sleep tonight. And bring that basket of vegetables with you. I didn't know about you being here and I meant them for Nigel.'

Gavin was beginning to feel frightened of her. She was nearly so very perceptive. He was thankful to pick up the basket and start across the courtyard with her.

Nigel came to the door when Barbara knocked on it. He looked a little aghast when he saw her, but then managed to produce an unconvincing smile. He thanked her when she thrust the basket of vegetables at him.

'This is really very good of you, Barbara,' he said. 'Is it just by chance you're here, or is it because you've heard of our troubles?'

'Of course it's because I've heard of them,' she answered in her harsh, abrupt way. 'Would I have got up at five this morning to catch an early train to London and another on to Tolcaster and then a taxi to Upthorn—my God, what a journey! I'd never have done it if it hadn't been a crisis— but you know that in a time of crisis you can count on me. I've been discussing it all with Gavin. If you shot the woman, Nigel, you needn't worry about my guessing it. Even if I'm not your wife who can't be compelled to give evidence against you, I am your sister and though we may not always see eye to eye about things, I wouldn't give you away.'

'But I haven't shot anybody!' The chilly smile with which Nigel had greeted her broadened into one of genuine amusement. 'Anyway, we needn't have it out on the doorstep. Come in and tell me how things are with you.'

He led her and Gavin into the drawing-room.

The door on to the terrace was closed and the room was in a mess. The fingerprint men had left their dust behind them and no doubt, Gavin thought, it would stay where it was until Mrs Nevin had gone to work on it. Chairs had been moved and left standing at odd angles. There were a number of footmarks on the fine old carpet. The flowers that were in a vase on top of a bookcase were shrivelled and dead. There was a musty smell of staleness in the room. It could hardly have been more depressing.

'You haven't brought any luggage,' Nigel said to Barbara.

'It's over at the cottage,' Gavin answered. He went to the terrace door and flung it open to let air into the room. 'We haven't decided if she's staying with me or with you. Do you want to stay at the cottage again tonight, Nigel, because if you do it would probably be best for Barbara to stay at an hotel. Does that pub in Upthorn let rooms, by any chance?'

'It does, but of course she can stay with you,' Nigel said. 'I was going to tell you I'd stay here anyway. I've got to get used to it sometime and I may as well start doing that straight away before I get too frightened of it. I can imagine it steadily getting worse if I don't make up my mind to face it.'

'Like falling off a horse,' Barbara said. 'I believe the right thing to do is to get straight on to it again. And I believe it's the same if you've crashed an aeroplane. Very sensible of you, but I don't mind staying here if you'd like me to.' She had sat down on the sofa where Gavin remembered Annabel and Marion Jay sitting side by side when the Jays had arrived for dinner. 'I've been asking Gavin if he thinks Caroline was blackmailing you, Nigel. He didn't actually offer any opinion on the subject.'

'Ah, so that's why I shot her, is it?' Nigel said. 'You really ought to have gone into the police instead of wasting your time flower-farming.'

'I did think of that before my marriage, you know,' she said. 'Only my health wouldn't have been up to it. Irregular hours, unwholesome food in wretched cafés and pubs, taking orders from mental defectives, because that's what

I'm sure a lot of them must be—I'd have been a nervous wreck in no time. Apart from that, I might have found the work interesting. But was she blackmailing you, Nigel?'

'Actually, no,' he answered.

'Because she must have known a great deal about you.'

'Oh, everything.' He sounded quite good-humoured about it. It was almost as if her questioning was cheering him up.

'And she never tried to make you pay for it?'

'Extorting money with menaces? No, that wasn't her line.'

'What was her line, then? Why did she give up her career and come to live with you? Do you think she could have been blackmailing Annabel?'

'I rather doubt it.'

'You aren't taking me seriously,' she said reprovingly. 'I only want to help. Don't you think Caroline may have had some hold on Annabel?'

'Nigel—' Gavin suddenly interrupted. He had been wandering about the room, absent-mindedly straightening the furniture. 'What are these?'

He had come on a collection of audio-cassettes piled on each other at the end of a bookshelf. His first thought about them was that they might be the tapes of Annabel's last books about which Mrs Nevin had told him, but when he looked at one or two of them he saw that they were not Annabel's works at all, but were some novels of Trollope's, of Thackeray's and of Agatha Christie's.

'Did Annabel listen to these?' he asked. 'Didn't she care for reading any more?'

'She couldn't read, however much she wanted to,' Nigel answered. 'As a matter of fact, she did want to very badly. It made her furious that she couldn't. She was blind as a bat, poor thing, for the last year or two. Her long sight was pretty good still, but even with very strong glasses her short sight had absolutely gone. That's why she was so clumsy about some things, like eating at meals. She was terrified that people would notice how she fumbled with her knife and fork. She said it was so humiliating.'

'And that's why you did her typing for her,' Gavin said. 'She dictated the stuff on to tape and you typed it because she didn't want to let on even to a professional typist that she couldn't see to do it herself.'

'My dear chap, she never dictated a word,' Nigel said. 'I wrote the whole of those two last bloody books myself, every word of them. And they brought in just as much money as anything she'd ever written.'

'*You* wrote two books for her!' Barbara exclaimed.

'I did indeed.'

'Then wasn't that what Caroline was blackmailing you *both* about?' Barbara cried. 'She knew it and she could have told the whole story to Annabel's publishers.'

'Who couldn't have cared less,' Nigel said. 'As long as the books sounded as if they'd been written by Annabel and had her signature on the contracts, it really didn't matter to them who'd actually written them.'

'Her signature,' Gavin said. 'She could see well enough to sign her name, could she?'

'Oh yes, most people can do that with their eyes shut. She could easily sign her name, though I don't suppose she could actually read what she was signing.'

'So when she signed her will, she may not have known what was in it.'

'I've been wondering when someone would think of that,' Nigel said. 'I may have got away with much more than she wanted me to.'

CHAPTER 7

'Why did you do it?' Gavin asked.

'Fake the will?' Nigel said.

'No, write the books. You couldn't have needed the money.'

'She wanted me to do it. At first it was almost a joke. She didn't believe it was possible. But then she began to think that if the image of Annabel Astor could be kept alive for a time, she'd like it. Of course she believed that she'd get back to writing herself sooner or later. So we went ahead with the thing and we always discussed everything as we went along, but all her plots were more or less the same and so were her characters, so if I stuck to one or two of her old books but changed names and colours of hair and so on there wasn't much I had to invent. Sometimes I'd get a bit carried away and make her characters start talking sense, but she always spotted it and pulled me up. And remember I'd been reading her books for twenty years. I'd always had to read her typescript when a book was finished and I'd thoroughly soaked up her style. The only difficulties arose when those two I did were as successful as usual. She got a bit jealous about that and started thinking the joke wasn't such a good one after all.'

'Didn't any reviewer spot the difference?' Barbara asked.

'Oh, Annabel's books never got reviewed,' Nigel said. 'They just sold in large quantities to the libraries and in paperback and were serialized in women's magazines, but I can't remember ever seeing a review. She sometimes got very upset when she saw the odd note somewhere just saying "Another Annabel Astor", but she somehow persuaded herself not to worry too much as long as the cheques kept rolling in.'

'About her will,' Gavin said, 'Caroline wrote it, did she?'

'Yes, she actually typed it,' Nigel replied.

'And cut herself out?'

'Yes, she did that.'

'I don't believe you,' Barbara said. 'It doesn't seem natural.'

'You don't think it's natural for a person not to be greedy?'

'What strikes me is that if Annabel had died intestate, Caroline might have got the whole lot,' she said. 'You'd no right to any of it. And I don't suppose Annabel's first husband would have risked trying to claim it. So Caroline was really giving a great deal away.'

'She knew I'd look after her, however things fell out.'

'It seems to me you were very sure Annabel was going to die sometime soon. Mightn't she in fact have lived for years, in which case your plotting wouldn't have done you any good.'

Nigel's face changed. A drawn look, a look of great sadness appeared on it.

'That's quite true,' he said. 'And if only that had happened! But you couldn't live with her and see the change in her and believe she'd still got long. Most people believed that the fact that she could go on writing meant she was in a fair way to recovery, but I knew the truth about that. And Desmond Jay told me on the quiet that I ought to be prepared for worst. But you've got me tagged as Caroline's murderer, haven't you, Barbara? Even if you can't dredge up a good motive for it, it's what you want to believe. In our charming family, it's the normal way for us to think of one another. Gavin, I believe you were in your living-room at the time of the murder. Did you happen to see me come or go?'

'No,' Gavin said.

'Mind you, I might not actually have driven up to the house,' Nigel said. 'I could have left my car in the lane and walked in. You're sure you didn't see me?'

'Quite sure.'

'Well, Barbara, what do you make of that?' Nigel asked. 'Do you think I'm gifted with occasional invisibility?'

'Of course not, and I'm not saying you must have murdered Caroline,' Barbara said, 'but I think it's best to explore every avenue, for your own sake as well as anything else. But as for Gavin saying he didn't see you, of course he'd say that, because you're the older brother he's always hero-worshipped. Actually, I'd do the same myself.'

'You aren't implying you've ever hero-worshipped me, are you?' Nigel said. 'I've never noticed it.'

'Certainly not, but I'd sooner not have you arrested for murder, and I think you ought to understand the difficulties of your position.'

'What makes you think I don't? But the fact is, Gavin is telling the truth when he says he didn't see me.'

'Didn't you see *anyone*, Gavin?' Barbara asked.

'Only the man with the Mercedes,' Gavin said, 'and I didn't see him arrive—'

He broke off because the telephone rang.

Nigel went out of the room to answer it. Barbara sat frowning as they heard him talking in the hall, then she repeated her question.

'You really didn't see anyone?'

'No, but I was sitting on the window-seat with my back to the window for a while,' Gavin answered. 'Then I was talking to Helena on the telephone. Whoever came, I didn't see him.'

'What about that girl who came to see you in the morning?' she said. 'Mightn't she have walked across the courtyard to the house from the cottage?'

'With murder in mind, knowing that I was in the cottage and able to see her go? Wouldn't that have been taking rather a risk, even for the most determined murderer?'

'Well, yes, it would have been. But someone came in, you must admit that.'

Nigel returned from the hall.

'It was Desmond,' he said. 'He suggested that we should go over there for lunch. Marion's worrying because she doesn't think we'll cook ourselves anything. I accepted.'

'But not for me!' Barbara exclaimed. 'I've never even met them.'

'Yes, I explained about you being here and Desmond said of course you must come too,' Nigel said. 'And I can assure you the food won't all have come out of tins, as it would if you stayed here. Marion even grows her own vegetables and has a herb-garden.'

Barbara gave an exasperated sigh. 'I'm so tired. The last thing I want is to have to speak politely to a lot of complete strangers.'

'I've never known you bother to speak politely to anyone,' Nigel said, 'so why start now? Come along, we'd better be going.'

They started out into the lane.

Nigel strode ahead and Gavin followed with Barbara. The day had become very warm, but there were some dark clouds moving across the sky which reminded Gavin of Inspector Frost's forecast that it would rain in the afternoon. He wondered if there might even be thunder presently. It felt to him as if there were thunder in the air, yet this could have been something internal, a sense of something threatening that was privately affecting his own nervous system as much as in the humid heat of the day. The door of the Jays' house was standing open when they reached it and Desmond Jay was waiting for them on the threshold.

Nigel introduced Barbara to him and they all went inside

and were given drinks, whisky for Nigel, sherry for Gavin and orange juice for Barbara. Leslie and Oliver Penbury were in the drawing-room when they went into it and Marion came hurrying in a moment later, with apologies for having been busy in the kitchen. The room was a big one with a high ceiling and tall windows, a good deal of cretonne everywhere and a few surprisingly valuable-looking pieces of antique furniture, a china cupboard with some fine china in it, a Regency sofa table, some chairs that might be Heppelwhite. Gavin remembered that Leslie worked in an antique shop in Tolcaster and thought that it was probably she who had chosen these things. The result was cheerful and comfortable and a bit of a muddle.

'You know, I'm very sorry I was so little help to you yesterday,' Desmond Jay said when they were all settled with their drinks. 'It was that cricket match. I didn't come here for lunch, but went straight to the field as soon as I was free. Then I thought I'd be more use going to the morgue to find out what was happening than coming over to you when you were probably flooded with the police anyway. Are they any farther on with things yet?'

'If so, they haven't told us,' Nigel replied. 'They're trying to trace a mysterious stranger whom Gavin saw come out of the house just before he went across to it himself and found . . .' He shrugged his shoulders and did not finish the sentence.

Gavin was thinking that, like the rest of the people there, Desmond Jay had no satisfactory alibi. He had had his medical duties to attend to in the morning and had spent the afternoon with his cricketing friends, but what had happened in between? And Marion had been alone in the house when Gavin had come here, unless Leslie had been in it. Yet Marion had not called her which suggested that perhaps she had not been at home. Where she might have been he did not know. Only Oliver Penbury, who had answered the telephone when Marion had called him, had a definite alibi. Nigel had been alone, claiming to have been sitting thinking in that lay-by. And Gavin himself had been alone.

Barbara and Marion had begun to talk about Marion's herb-garden. Barbara offered her advice on the use of compost and the terrible results that might be caused by the use of chemical fertilizers. Nigel asked Desmond Jay what the fate of Upthorn had been in the cricket match. It appeared that they had suffered ignominious defeat at the hands of Nether Thorn. Leslie and Oliver seemed to be engrossed in a low-voiced conversation. It was plain that it had been decided that there should be as little talk as possible about death, natural or unnatural.

Gavin, left more or less to himself, began to brood on something that had not occurred to him before and that was the probability, indeed almost the certainty, that the murderer had been in the Cleavers' house when he himself had been in it. Otherwise surely he would have seen this person leave. If whoever it was had entered the house when Gavin had been sitting with his back to the window or been talking on the telephone, the murderer might have arrived without being seen, but could hardly have left invisibly. So that must mean that he had either been the man with the Mercedes or had remained in the house while first that man, then Gavin, had been there, and had escaped while Gavin had made his frantic dash for help to the Jays' house. What would have happened, he wondered, if he had more sensibly telephoned the police on the spot? Possibly the police would have found three corpses when they arrived.

There was roast beef and blackberry and apple pie for lunch and afterwards there was coffee in the drawing-room. Talking seemed to be a great effort to everyone and Nigel was almost completely silent. Yet it was he who abruptly broke through the barrier of polite platitudes with an announcement.

'I'm thinking of going to Australia.'

Desmond Jay said, 'What?'

Marion said, 'Nigel!'

Leslie said, 'Ah!' as if this were something for which she had been waiting.

Neither Barbara nor Oliver said anything.

Nigel, holding his coffee-cup, began to roam around the room.

'It's been on my mind for some time, actually,' he said. 'If it hadn't been for Annabel's love for the place I don't suppose I'd have stayed on as long as I have. And I've faced the fact for some time that sooner or later I'd have to decide what I'd do with myself when I lost her. I knew that might not happen for years, but also I knew it could happen any day. And the one thing I knew was that I'd never be able to stay in that house alone. Even if there hadn't been the ghastly sort of disaster there that there has been, I'd have had to leave. I'm sure you all understand that.'

'Only too well!' Leslie muttered. She was smiling with a look of ironic satisfaction and Gavin remembered what she had said to him about Nigel remaining in Upthorn only because of Annabel and his dependence on her, that but for her he would long ago have left for London, and had she not mentioned New York and Sydney? Now she seemed to feel a mocking sort of satisfaction in having been proved right.

'Of course we understand you'll want to leave the house,' Desmond Jay said, 'but what about your job? You don't want to walk out on the Cantlewell, do you?'

'Why not?' Nigel asked.

'Well, it's quite an important job, and I always thought it meant a good deal to you,' Jay said.

'So it did for a time,' Nigel replied, 'but to tell the truth, I've been bored with it for years. Perhaps it's the way we were brought up in my family, always on the move from one place to another, but it's never felt natural to me, getting stuck in one place for years. You'll find it had the opposite effect on Gavin. He wouldn't feel safe if he hadn't dug himself into that bloody school where he teaches and where he's going to stay for the rest of his life. But I've had the itch to get moving for a long time.'

'But of course you couldn't, could you, unless Annabel agreed?' Leslie said. 'She could dictate to you, couldn't she?'

She still wore her ironic smile and there was a strange degree of malice in her voice.

Nigel looked at her without expression. 'Yes, she could dictate things,' he said, 'but not simply because she happened to have the money, which is what you mean, isn't it, Leslie dear? I know only too well what you think of me. I was ready to stay here because she happened to love it and I stuck to my job because I didn't want to be entirely dependent on her.'

'But now the money's yours and you can't wait to get away,' Leslie said. 'And you said yourself, you've had it planned for some time. So all in all, things haven't fallen out too badly for you. It's just rather a pity about Caroline.'

'Leslie, how can you say such a thing?' Marion cried, her face pale and shocked. 'You're almost accusing Nigel of— of wanting poor Annabel's death.'

'Isn't that what he's almost said himself?' Leslie said.

'I doubt if anyone else has interpreted what I said in that way,' Nigel said.

'I wouldn't be too sure of that.'

That Nigel and Leslie were having a fierce little quarrel was something of which Gavin was aware and thought that it must be equally obvious to everyone else in the room. Oliver Penbury was gazing blankly in front of him, avoiding looking at anybody, but one corner of his mouth was pulled down in an odd little grimace. He had picked up a spoon and was going on and on stirring his coffee with it. Desmond Jay was frowning.

Marion looked almost on the edge of starting to cry. Barbara looked unmoved but suddenly got to her feet.

'Mrs Jay, about your herb-garden,' she said, 'I should be so interested to see it. Would you perhaps show it to me?'

Gavin was unaccustomed to tact from Barbara, but thought that for once he must give her full marks.

'Why, of course,' Marion said, also getting hastily to her feet. 'You're interested in such things, of course. I do so love being able to use things straight out of our garden, instead of the horrid dried-up things from shops. Do come along.'

The two women left the room together.

'But you're serious about giving up your job, are you, Nigel?' Jay asked.

'I'm going to write my letter of resignation tomorrow,' Nigel said.

'And what will you do in Australia?'

'I haven't the faintest idea.'

'Of course, you can—well, take your time before you decide on anything.' Jay did not quite like to say that with the money that would be his, Nigel could settle down to do nothing indefinitely, if that was what he chose. 'But you can't leave immediately. You'll have to wait till this horrible business here has been sorted out.'

'Yes.'

'If you don't like staying alone in that house, you could move in with us.'

'That's very good of you, Desmond, but I'll be all right.'

He did not look quite all right. He looked more tense, more strained than when he, Gavin and Barbara had arrived. Gavin thought that it would have been best if the Jays' invitation to lunch had not been accepted and that they had reconciled themselves to the eternal bread and cheese at home.

He turned to Leslie.

'I've been wondering about something, Leslie,' he said. 'When you were with me yesterday morning, sitting in that easy chair, did you see anyone arrive at the house?'

'The police have already asked me that,' she answered. 'I saw the Mercedes turn in at the gate and a man get out of it and go up to the house. But he wasn't anyone I knew and I didn't pay much attention to him. He went to the front door and then when he didn't get an answer he went on to the terrace and disappeared. I supposed he was simply a visitor Annabel and Caroline were expecting.'

'And you didn't see anybody else?'

'No.'

'You see, a thing that's been puzzling me is that whoever got into the house and shot Caroline can't have known that I was in the cottage and that by sheer chance I shouldn't see him go into the house, or they'd never have taken the risk of going there.'

'Now that's a very interesting point!' Jay exclaimed. 'Yes, indeed. And all of us in here knew you were there and so did Mrs Nevin and Jim Boyce. In fact, it was probably all around the village. To tell you the truth, Nigel, I believe you're going to have to face the fact, like it or not, that it was Annabel who went out of her mind and shot Caroline.'

Nigel sat down abruptly, put his elbows on his knees and his face in his hands. As he sat there without saying anything, Jay uneasily cleared his throat and after a moment said, 'Of course, I don't mean . . .'

But he did not try to say what he had not meant and with a sudden shudder Nigel dropped his hands but did not look up. When he spoke he might have been addressing the carpet at his feet.

'I know that's how it looks,' he said, 'except for there

being no fingerprints on the gun and nothing in the way of a cloth or gloves or anything else near her to show how she might have cleaned it up before collapsing. And in a way I can't help wishing we could explain that and be sure she did this thing, because neither she nor anyone else would have to pay for it. If she did do it, we know she wasn't in her right mind and shouldn't be blamed for it and we could stop the horrible business of trying to pin the guilt on anyone else.'

'Isn't it obvious they've got to find the man with the Mercedes?' Leslie said. 'I saw him come and Gavin saw him leave, and that means he'd plenty of time in the house to kill Caroline. And he's probably someone we've never even heard of. We were all puzzled, weren't we, at Caroline giving up her acting and staying here, but suppose it was simply to get away from that man. Suppose she'd been somehow involved with him and had got dead scared of him and ran away from him. And that Annabel collapsed when she did could have been because he frightened her, or it could have been sheer coincidence. And it was just a mistake on his part taking away whatever he'd used to clean the gun instead of leaving it by her body.'

'How did he know where to find the gun?' Gavin asked.

No one answered that at once. Then Jay said, 'You know, Annabel could have held the gun wrapped in her skirt after cleaning off the prints left on it by herself and Nigel the evening before. Isn't that possible?'

Again no one answered and after a pause he muttered, 'No, perhaps it isn't likely.'

'So the situation is,' Nigel said, 'that the only people who knew where the gun was are the people who've been here today, but it happens that all those people know that Gavin was in the cottage and could probably see them come and go. So that doesn't make sense, does it?'

Oliver Penbury joined diffidently in the discussion. 'You

know, I think she's right, it must have been the strange man. If he got into the house and somehow threatened Caroline and she got out the gun to defend herself and he managed to get it away from her and shot her, and then he threatened Annabel with it and she simply fell and died without his having to shoot her, wouldn't that make sense?'

'Except that the police say there were no signs that Caroline had been in any kind of a struggle,' Gavin said, 'and when I went into the kitchen and found her she appeared to have been sitting peacefully at the table, reading a cookery book.'

'So it must have been Annabel who did it,' Nigel said, still looking down at the floor between his feet. 'I think it would be best for all of us if we agreed on that. Perhaps it means that the guilty will go unpunished but does that really matter? Isn't the world a stinking sewer of guilt? What's a little here or there?' He stood up. 'Desmond, I think we'd better be going. I wonder if you could rescue Marion from Barbara's clutches in the garden.'

The two women were called in and a few minutes later Nigel, Gavin and Barbara started on the short walk home.

Barbara was in good spirits. She had been enjoying herself.

'That's a very nice, intelligent woman,' she remarked. 'All considered, she's made a pretty good thing of her garden. I was able to give her a little advice which I think she'll find useful, but I was glad to see she'd an excellent compost heap. Very fortunate for her family that they're getting good fresh things from the garden all the time. I liked her very much.'

There was no one Barbara liked so much as someone to whom she had been able to give advice. She talked on happily about the herbs that Marion grew and the high standard of her lettuces, peas and raspberries while both Nigel and Gavin remained silent. When they reached the house a few drops of rain were starting to fall and the sky had grown dark and threatening. They were about to enter the house when Barbara pointed out that her suitcase was still in the cottage and that it had not yet been settled where she was to sleep.

'You'd better stay in the cottage,' Nigel said. 'You can have the room I had last night. As I said before, I've got to get used to being alone in the house till I can get right away from it.'

'To Australia?' she asked. 'You really meant that?'

'Or it might be New York or South America,' he answered. 'That's unimportant. But my letter of resignation to the Cantlewell gets written tomorrow. Now I'd better go over to the cottage and collect the things I left there last night.'

He went with Gavin and Barbara round the courtyard, carried Barbara's suitcase upstairs for her into the room where he had slept the night before, collected the belongings that he had left there, then left her to unpack and to have the wash that she said she wanted, and joined Gavin in the living-room.

But instead of leaving at once, Nigel sat down on the window-seat and took his head in his hands again as he had at the Jays'.

'I pretty much gave things away, didn't I?' he said. 'You've guessed the truth, I imagine.'

'If you mean that Leslie was the woman you had your affair with,' Gavin answered, 'yes, I admit I did.'

'I ought to have controlled myself better,' Nigel said.

'I don't think she cared much. She wanted a chance to quarrel with you. I don't think she'd have minded a blazing row.'

'That's how it's always been. It's why I had to put a stop to it. I was turning into something I didn't much like. I've never got much of a kick out of quarrelling, allowing for having running battles with Barbara and Helena, but they never amounted to anything.'

'It was you who broke it off, was it?'

'Yes, although she'd been asking for it for some time. For one thing, she was trying to break things up between me and Annabel, which wasn't my idea at all.'

'Did she know you weren't actually married?'

'Yes, I was fool enough to tell her.'

'The first time I met her she told me she wanted to be married and have two children.'

'That was the trouble, she did, so I had to make it final.'

'So you asked me down here to inhabit the cottage to do just that.'

Nigel raised his head from his hands and gave Gavin a wry smile.

'I should have known you'd realize that sooner or later. You were always too shrewd for me. Yes, we used to meet here once our last tenants left and it was only when Leslie discovered that the place wasn't going to be available any more that she really took in that I meant what I said about our breaking things off.'

'What about Penbury?' Gavin asked. 'Does he know about it?'

Nigel gave a slight shrug of his shoulders. 'After this afternoon I imagine he must have caught on. Before that, I'm not sure. Leslie said he hadn't any suspicion, but she's an uninhibited liar.'

'That's what she said about you.'

'And there I expect you now think she was telling the truth.'

'Is she really engaged to Penbury?'

'I rather doubt it.'

'Marion said she thought they were, but didn't sound too sure about it.'

'Of course she and Desmond wish they were, but they can tell the situation isn't exactly simple.'

'You think they know about you?'

'If they do, it doesn't seem to have changed their friendship for me, though that could have been on Annabel's account. They were very good to her. They wouldn't have wanted to do anything to make her life more difficult. But I'm inclined to think they really didn't know. They'd think I was a bit too old for anything between Leslie and me to be serious when there was Oliver around.'

'Though she isn't exactly a child.'

'She hasn't been one for a long time. She acquired her maturity early.'

'If only I understood where Caroline fits into this whole thing.' Gavin had thrown himself down in the easy chair.

'Do you mean you really haven't understood that?'

Gavin found Nigel's dark eyes fastened on his face with a half-mocking stare.

'If you're thinking of . . .' Gavin began, then broke it off.

'Well, that isn't impossible, is it? Though there are one or two things I can't make sense of,' Nigel replied. 'And but for one thing, after all, I'm far the best suspect myself. Caroline faked that will for me, letting Annabel think it was just another contract she was signing, but as things are I can afford to spend my time going round and round the world if I can't think of anything better to do with myself.'

'But that one thing you mentioned that spoils the theory is that neither Leslie nor I saw you arrive at the house,' Gavin said.

'Only suppose Leslie did,' Nigel suggested. 'Have you considered that? I told you she's a liar.'

Gavin had a feeling that some question that he had asked had been dodged, but he was not sure what it was.

'You think she still cares enough for you to risk telling that particular lie?' he asked.

'I'm not sure, but she might,' Nigel said.

'Are you telling me that you did come to the house yesterday morning?'

'Certainly not.' Nigel stood up. 'I'm just playing with hypotheses. In the end I suspect Desmond's right and we'll settle for the probability that Annabel did that shooting. There's no danger from the dead.'

'I wonder,' Gavin said. 'I wonder if there isn't.'

The brothers exchanged a long look, each trying to penetrate what was passing in the mind of the other. Gavin realized that he did not know quite what he himself had meant.

Just then there were heavy footsteps on the stairs and Barbara thrust her way into the room.

'I've just had an excellent idea,' she said. 'If you're seriously thinking of leaving your house, Nigel, why don't I take it over from you?'

He looked at her in astonishment. She dropped down on a chair and smiled up at him.

'What in the world do you mean?' he asked.

'Just what I said,' she answered. 'I'll take it over from you and I'll turn it into a guest-house. It's perfectly suited for it. Of course there would have to be some modifications made to it, but really one couldn't want anything better.'

'Probably you couldn't,' he agreed, 'but where are you going to get the money to buy it?'

'Money?' she said as if it were something of which she had never heard.

'Money,' he said firmly. 'I expect to get thousands for it, perhaps even some hundreds of thousands. You've nothing like that sort of money yourself, have you?'

'You know I haven't,' she said with dignity. 'But if you want it to be commercial, it seems to me you could regard it as an investment.'

'I certainly want it to be commercial.'

'In that case, we could have a contract about it, all signed and sealed. I would pay you rent and you would get a percentage of the profits. You would certainly get a very good rate of interest on your capital. The people who came would get really good food. We could dig up most of the garden and grow our own vegetables and the courtyard could easily be turned into a splendid run for free-range chickens. And if we needed to take on any extra staff, as I suppose we should, they could sleep in this cottage. And everything we gave the people would be fresh and good and not fattening and they'd soon spread the word about it and we'd get well known. We might advertise in a few of the right sort of magazines. We'd say we could cater for special diets. You know, I've always wanted to undertake something like that, but I've never seen just the right place for it. But this house would be perfect, don't you think so yourself?'

'What about those modifications you mentioned?' Nigel said. 'I suppose you mean half a dozen bathrooms and a bit of modernizing in the kitchen and so on. Who's going to pay for all that?'

'I thought I might manage that,' she answered.

'Good of you,' he said.

'Well, if I sold my house in Devon, you see, I'd probably get quite a good price for it and that would probably be enough to cover the improvements. I've been trying to decide whether it would be best to make the place a simple guest-house, taking people for relatively short visits, or if one mightn't do better by making it a retirement home for the elderly. They're badly needed nowadays, with people living longer and longer. But it would be more expensive converting the place for them. One might even have to enlarge it. And they'd need a library, for instance, and a laundry, and perhaps hairdressing facilities.'

'And a bar,' Nigel said. 'Don't forget the bar. You'd have

to get a licence. Old people like to have their comfortable drink of an evening.'

'Then you think it's a good idea,' she said, as usual missing the irony in his tone and believing that he was beginning to take an interest in her suggestion. 'Not that we'd have a bar. As you know, I don't hold with the drinking that goes on nowadays. Don't you think we might discuss the matter with your friend Desmond Jay, because of course if we went in for an old people's home we'd need a doctor in attendance? Or we might ask the opinion of that young doctor, Oliver Penbury—wasn't that his name? Though I know all either of them would do is prescribe pills, just bottles and bottles of pills, unnatural chemical things, when the whole point of what I want to do is to give people really wholesome food to eat, not poisoned by a lot of fertilizers and God knows what else. You must admit there's something inspiring about the whole conception. The more I think of it, the better I like it. What do you think, Gavin?'

Gavin had intended to keep out of the discussion. He enjoyed good food but was generally ready to eat anything that was put in front of him. Having spent as much of his life as he had in a boarding-school for boys, he was ready to take the rough with the smooth. He did not reply to Barbara's question and Nigel was gentler with her than he had expected.

'You must give me a little time to think it over,' he said.

But perhaps this was not really as kind as it sounded. Since it was certain that he would not give even the briefest consideration to Barbara's proposal, it might have been less brutal to have nipped the idea in the bud immediately.

'Naturally,' she said and looked pleased. 'One should never take important decisions when one has too much else on one's mind. Oh look—you've got a visitor!'

She was looking out of the window. As she spoke a taxi

circled the courtyard and came to a stop outside the cottage door. The door of the taxi opened and a slim, red-haired woman stepped out of it.

Nigel clenched both fists, raised them above his head and shook them in rage at the universe. It was as if all of a sudden he had had more than he could bear.

'No!' he shouted. 'Christ, no, it can't be!'

But it was. It was Helena.

CHAPTER 8

Gavin went out to help her with her suitcase. She smiled at him but did not kiss him. She looked frail and not very well, but that was how she had always looked. With age her pretty, delicate features were beginning to look pinched. Her red hair, now streaked with grey, hung in a tangled mass round her face in what happened to be the fashion of the moment. She was wearing neat emerald green trousers and a shirt to match.

As the taxi drove off a rumble of thunder sounded faintly in the distance. The rain was falling more heavily now and she made a hasty dash for the doorway.

Seeing Nigel and Barbara in the room, she stood still and exclaimed unhappily, 'Oh Lord, I didn't realize we'd all be here!'

Gavin had followed her in with her suitcase. He closed the door.

'I believe this is the first time the whole family's been gathered together for years,' he said. 'I can't remember when it last happened.'

'It just shows what a little murder will do,' Nigel observed. 'Hallo, Helena, nice to see you.'

'You weren't expecting me, of course,' she said.

'I was,' Barbara said. 'I didn't think you'd be able to resist it.'

'Resist what?' Helena said. 'The chance to stay here quietly with Gavin for a while? No, I admit I was tempted. I don't really care for staying with him in Stillborough because of the noise those awful children downstairs keep making, but I've always enjoyed staying with him from time to time. He understands me better than any of the rest of you. But what are you doing here? Family gatherings have never been much in your line.'

Barbara turned to Nigel. 'I believe she doesn't know what's happened.'

'Has anything happened?' Helena asked. 'Anything special?'

'You don't watch television,' Nigel said.

'No, as a matter of fact, I don't,' she answered. 'I haven't even got a set. Such rubbish as they dish out to one! Take that serial, *For Ever and a Day*—'

'And you don't read the newspapers,' he interrupted her.

'Not very often.' She began to look nervous. 'Something *has* happened. I can feel it. You may not want to tell me what it is, but I can feel it. Something terrible. It's in all your faces.'

'It really takes genius to arrive at that, doesn't it?' Barbara said. 'All that's happened, Helena, is a sudden death and a murder. We're all rather upset about it.'

'Ah,' Helena said, 'I knew it had to be something like that. I felt it as soon as I came into the room. But whose death? Whose murder? Please tell me.'

'You didn't feel a bloody thing when you came in,' Barbara growled. 'You were just fed up at seeing us gathered together here before you.'

'Oh, you're always so horrid to me.' Helena sounded as if she were going to cry. 'I did feel something at once . . . Gavin, please tell me what's happened.'

Sooner than allowing the two sisters to develop one of their customary brawls which in childhood had led them to screaming and throwing things at one another but which in maturity had changed to mere rudeness and the desire to wound one another verbally as much as possible, Gavin tried in as few words as he could to acquaint Helena with what had happened there during the last two days.

He began, 'I'm afraid Annabel's dead.'

'Annabel?' Helena exclaimed. 'Oh, Nigel, I'm so sorry.'

'But that isn't the whole story,' Gavin went on. 'Nigel wasn't joking when he mentioned murder. You remember Caroline, Annabel's younger sister? Well, around the time Annabel died, Caroline died too, but it happens she was killed by being shot in the head. The police have been here, and the television people, and the press, and they're pretty sure it was murder, though there's just a very faint possibility it was suicide. But I don't think anyone believes in that.'

Helena subsided on to the window-seat, from which Nigel had got up when she came in.

'Oh God, I'm so sorry,' she said. 'I'd never have come bursting in like that if I'd known. Why didn't you telephone, Gavin? You knew I was coming. Now I'll only be in the way—unless I can help. Perhaps I can help. Of course they suspect Nigel of having done it.'

'Thank you,' Nigel said. 'It's so obvious I'm a murderer, is it?'

She gave him a long, thoughtful look, but only said, 'Go on, tell me the rest of it. There must be a lot more you haven't told me yet. For instance, how did Annabel die? Was she murdered too?'

'They think not,' Gavin said. 'They think it was a second cerebral haemorrhage and she just collapsed and died.'

'Pure coincidence?' she asked. 'I don't like coincidences. They nearly always have a meaning, make part of a pattern. We're all linked to one another in some way.'

'Well, apart from suspecting me,' Nigel said, 'one of the things they suspect is that Annabel killed Caroline, then collapsed from the shock of what she had done. It's a convenient theory in some ways, because it explains why no one was seen arriving at the house except for a strange man who was seen to go in by a friend and whom Gavin saw leaving, but who couldn't have known where the gun that killed Caroline was kept. But look, we're much too crowded in here. Let's go across to the house and have some tea or something.'

'I'd like a drink, if you can manage that,' Helena said. 'That journey's tired me out and now the shock of hearing all this . . . Whisky, if you have it, Nigel.'

'I wonder how many drinks you had on the journey,' Barbara said. 'But don't worry, they're never out of whisky. There may not be a thing to eat in the house except what comes out of tins, but you can rely on the supply of alcohol. Come on, let's make a dash for it.'

She opened the door and plunged out into the now heavy rain.

Thunder rumbled, still in the distance but a little louder than before as they ran across the courtyard. Nigel opened the heavy oak door of the house and led them into the dining-room. He seemed to feel it was less contaminated by tragedy than the drawing-room, and also it was where the drinks were kept. He poured out a strong whisky for Helena and a tonic for Barbara and they both seated themselves at the table, facing one another, as if they were preparing for a particularly bitter argument about something or other. Gavin, also with a whisky, strolled to the window and stood there, gazing out at the pale curtain of rain. It had made a little puddle on the floor beneath the window where it had pattered in through the hole in the glass that had been shattered by Annabel's wild shot on Friday evening.

'There's something I've been wondering about, Nigel,' he said. 'Isn't there any way into the house except through that gate? Isn't there some back way in?'

'Not really,' Nigel answered. 'As you may have noticed, there's a high wooden fence right round the top of the garden. We put it there because sheep used to keep getting into it from the downs when we'd only a hedge. The police were interested in that and examined the fence pretty thoroughly, but there weren't any signs of someone having climbed it. And there's a flowerbed this side of it and there weren't any footmarks on it or any appearance of its having been disturbed.'

'So they're sticking to the idea that whoever killed Caroline must have come in through the gate,' Gavin said.

'Yes, unless it was Annabel.'

'Yes, of course, unless it was Annabel.'

'Tell me about this stranger who couldn't have known where the gun was kept,' Helena said.

Nigel told her the whole story again, this time in a good deal more detail than Gavin had told it. She listened with grave attention, occasionally giving a slight shake of her head as if she were rejecting something that he had said, though it might have been simply something that had crossed her mind.

Barbara interrupted by saying, 'Where's Helena going to sleep tonight?'

'She can sleep in the spare room,' Nigel said. 'We'd better make up the bed for her here.'

'Here, do you mean?' Helena asked. 'Here in this house?'

'Yes, there's plenty of room,' he answered.

'But surely I'm staying with Gavin,' she said. 'In the cottage.'

'No, Barbara's staying there,' Nigel explained.

'But I telephoned Gavin . . .' She broke off and looked from Nigel to Barbara. 'Well, let me look at this room upstairs,' she said.

'It's really quite a nice room,' he assured her. 'It'll do very well for one of Barbara's paying guests. All she'll have to do to it is put in a television and a fridge and some apparatus for making tea and coffee. The furniture will do as it is.'

'Barbara's paying guests!' Helena exclaimed. 'What *do* you mean?'

'He doesn't mean anything, he isn't serious,' Barbara said. 'He hasn't had time to think it over. We'll talk about it presently, when he has.'

'I don't understand,' Helena said helplessly. 'But let me look at the room. If I'm going to sleep there we'll have to fetch my suitcase from the cottage.'

She and Nigel went out of the room together.

After only two or three minutes they returned to it. Helena was slightly flushed.

'No,' she was saying definitely. 'I'm very sorry, Nigel, but I tell you, I couldn't sleep there. I can *feel* something . . . You know, I'm very sensitive in that sort of way and I can feel the evil in the house. It isn't surprising really, as murder's been done here, and it may stay for a long time unless you do something about it. There's a woman I know, a very gifted woman, whom I might be able to persuade to come here and help you, she's done some wonderful things, driving out that awful lingering evil that stays behind when dreadful things have been done.'

'For God's sake,' Barbara said, 'all you need is the local parson to come in with bell, book and candle and do a little exorcizing. I'm sure he'd oblige. What she means, Nigel, is simply that the thought of murder frightens her, which after all is quite natural, and she wants to run away from it as fast as she can. That evil you're talking about, Helena, is mostly in your own mind. There's no need to drag spirits or such things into it.'

'If it means so little to you, why don't you come and sleep over here?' Helena asked. 'Then I could stay at the cottage.'

'I've settled in at the cottage, thank you,' Barbara said. 'I don't want to have to pack up my things again.'

'You see?' Helena said, turning to Nigel. 'She may laugh at me. She always has. But she's frightened too, even if she doesn't feel things as I do.'

'I think what would be best all round,' Gavin said, 'is for me to move in here and for you two girls to stay at the cottage. What about it, Nigel?'

'Certainly,' Nigel said, 'if that'll give us a little peace. I'll be glad of your company. As I told you last night, I don't much like staying in the place alone myself. I'm afraid it's going to be haunted for me for a long time, perhaps for good. Whatever I finally decide to do, I shan't stay in it any longer than I've got to, though I dare say murder having happened here will bring its market value down. And don't you think it may keep those paying guests of yours away, Barbara, or your old people?'

'Paying guests, old people?' Helena said. 'I don't understand. I do wish you'd tell me what you're talking about.'

'It's just that Barbara thinks she'd like to take the place over and run it as a guest-house,' Nigel said. 'I'd call it a swift and certain way to bankruptcy, but she doesn't seem to think so. Now what shall we do about supper? We could make a salad with some of those things you brought yesterday, Barbara, and open a tin of ham.'

'I'll see to it,' Barbara said, standing up. 'I should think we can do better than that. Leave it to me.'

At that moment there was a knock at the front door.

Nigel gave a sigh of desperation. 'It'll be the police back again. I wonder what they want now.'

He was starting towards the door when Gavin, who was still at the window, said, 'No, it isn't the police. They don't arrive in a grey Mercedes.'

Nigel stood still, giving him a startled look. 'A grey Mercedes? Really?'

'Yes.'

'This is interesting.'

He quickly left the room and they heard him open the front door.

In a hushed voice, Helena said hurriedly, 'Of course, when I said there's evil in this house, I didn't mean Nigel. I hope you understood that. He isn't a murderer. I should know it if he were. He'd never be able to keep it from me.'

'I believe he could keep it from all of us if he felt inclined to do so,' Barbara said. 'He's always been able to deceive anyone he wanted to. A very clever actor in his way. He was wasted in a museum. He ought to have gone on the stage and married Caroline instead of Annabel.'

'But she'd have been far too young—' Helena broke off as Nigel ushered their visitor into the dining-room.

It was the man whom Gavin had seen fleeing from the house the day before. There was no question of that. His age might have been anything between sixty and seventy. He was tall and solidly built, with a sizeable paunch and the folds of a double chin under his heavy jaw. He was almost bald and the little hair that he had left was grey. His eyes were small and grey, under thick lids, his lips were thin and his cheeks were puffy. There was a frown on his broad forehead. He was wearing a very well-cut dark suit, a white shirt and a black tie, as if he were in mourning.

'Mr Halliday,' Nigel announced. 'My sisters, Mr Halliday, and my brother. I must confess we didn't expect you to turn up like this. You know the police are looking for you.'

'How could I help knowing it?' The man had the hoarse

voice of someone who smokes and drinks too much. 'Isn't it on every bloody television screen in the country?'

'Mr Halliday's Annabel's actual husband,' Nigel explained to the rest of his family. 'Her actual widower. Would you care for a drink, Mr Halliday?'

'Thanks.'

'Whisky?'

'Fine.'

'Then sit down and tell us to what we owe this unexpected visit. Is it by any chance to confess to a murder? Has it been weighing on your mind?'

'On my mind, yes. On my conscience, no.' The man sat down. 'I haven't committed any murder. I've nothing to confess, except that I've been a fool. I oughtn't to have lost my head and bolted. That was the act of a fool. But having done it, it's taken me some time to decide what I ought to do about it. I've guessed the police would catch up with me sooner or later. In the end I decided to give myself up.'

'But why here?' Nigel asked as he brought Jerome Halliday his drink. 'Why not to the police in Tolcaster? I'll have to let them know you've come.'

'I'd an idea I'd like to talk to you first,' the man replied. 'But go ahead and phone them if you want to.'

Nigel sat down at the table. 'What did you want to talk about?'

'Why I wanted to see Annabel. You or Annabel or both of you, it didn't matter which, though it's true I was looking forward to seeing her again after all these years. And if it turned out that the police didn't know the truth about your marriage, I didn't want to be the one to embarrass you.' He gestured at Barbara and Helena. 'I presume these ladies know it.'

'I've known if for perhaps an hour,' Helena said. 'I still haven't got used to the idea.'

'And I'm only a little in advance of her,' Barbara added.

'And my brother and the police have known it only since yesterday,' Nigel said. 'Annabel and I decided to keep the whole thing to ourselves. It wasn't of any importance to anybody.'

'I'm glad to hear you say that, immensely glad,' Halliday said. 'I've always thought Annabel was wonderfully generous and I wanted to thank her, in case it was important to her and to you, and tell her that there'd be no trouble now if you did want to go ahead and get married.'

'A little late in the day, isn't it?' Nigel said. 'It could hardly matter to us after all these years.'

'I realize that, but one doesn't know what a thing like that may mean to a person. Perhaps she'd been pining all these years to have the knot tied properly, and I wanted her to know that it was up to her now what she did about it. You understand how it all began, don't you?'

'More or less.'

'We'd been separated for ten years already, you see. No divorce, which was just casualness. Neither of us wanted the trouble with expense and the law courts and all that when we parted. I don't suppose either of us thought we were likely to get married again, or if we did, that that was the time when we could think about divorce. And what we didn't think of was that I'd go crazy about a woman who wouldn't have me except as a husband, and who was a Catholic at that and wouldn't marry me even if I'd had a divorce. So I kept quiet about having been married before and she and I got married in a church with all the trimmings and to the end of her life she never knew that marriage was bigamous.'

'The end of her life?' Gavin said. 'Do you mean she's dead now?'

'Died a month ago,' Halliday answered, absentmindedly fingering the black tie that he was wearing. 'And that's what I wanted to tell Annabel. It was her generosity, you see, that made that marriage possible. When we met by chance some years after we'd separated, I told her the whole situation, what I'd done, I mean, and how she could blow everything sky high for me if she went ahead with a divorce then. Of course, she'd every right to do it and get me in serious trouble too for bigamy. But she told me not to worry and later I heard she'd got married herself, so I naturally thought at first that was bigamy also and I wrote to her once—it's the only communication we've had since that other meeting of ours—and wished her luck and thanked her for what she'd done for me. And I got a short note back from her, just saying she hadn't committed bigamy at all and would I please keep out of her way. So I did.' He sipped some whisky then glanced at Nigel from under his heavy brows. 'None of this is news to you, is it? As I was saying, I just wanted to make sure of that before I went to the police.'

'No, Annabel didn't keep any of it from me,' Nigel said. 'In fact, we never married. But you haven't explained how Annabel and I could have got married without her committing bigamy, since you appear still to be alive.'

'Well, there'd be nothing now to stop her divorcing me, would there?' Halliday said. 'My dear wife's dead and wouldn't be hurt by it. That's what I came to tell Annabel.'

'Even at the risk of your being exposed as a bigamist,' Nigel said. 'I must say, that was rather heroic.'

A faint smile twisted the visitor's thin lips.

'I did talk it over with a lawyer friend of mine,' he said. 'He thought it was unlikely I'd run into much trouble about it, the original offence having been so far in the past, the results so satisfactory all round and my second wife being dead. And bigamy, he said, isn't taken so very seriously nowadays. So I thought I'd give Annabel a chance to achieve respectability at last, if she happened to want it. I admit I'd a certain curiosity to see her again after all these years. When I left her she wasn't a highly successful writer of romantic novels. She was a very shy, diffident sort of girl who felt she was a failure at everything. I've an idea that was partly my fault. I didn't mean to do it, but somehow I gave her that feeling.'

'Perhaps if you'd known what she was going to be, you wouldn't have left her,' Barbara said.

'Perhaps not,' he agreed with another of his tight little smiles.

Gavin thought about what this man must have been like at the time when he and Annabel had married. According to her, he had been very good at most sports and fond of fast cars, a quality that had probably seemed very glamorous to her when she was only nineteen. She had added that he was a bastard, though it was to be assumed that she had not recognized that immediately, but that he had been one was easier to imagine than that this heavy, portly man had ever been the slim, vigorous and no doubt dashingly handsome youth that he had been when she fell in love with him.

At the same time it was difficult to imagine Annabel as shy and diffident and suffering from a sense of being a failure. There had been very little of that left when Gavin had first met her. Perhaps this man had been right when he said that he had been at least partly responsible for it by being too overpoweringly gifted at things that mean so much to the young. In that case it might be that his leaving her had been the best thing that could have happened to her. But Gavin remembered her occasional moods of self-mockery and wondered if these could have been her way of concealing traces of the old feeling of inadequacy.

Brilliant light suddenly blazed in the room, followed only an instant later by a long, rumbling crash of thunder.

'Getting nearer,' Jerome Halliday observed.

Rain was drumming with monotonous force on the window-panes and the puddle under the window was growing larger.

'We ought to be phoning the police,' Barbara said.

'But Mr Halliday still hasn't told us what he found when he came here yesterday,' Nigel said. 'I'd like to hear about that.'

'You probably know as well as I do,' Halliday said, 'unless someone changed things after I'd been in. I tried knocking at the door, as I did just now, but got no answer. I was thinking of going away when it struck me that there might be some other way into the house and I wandered round and found that door in from the terrace. It was open, so I stood there, shouting, "Annabel!" But there still wasn't any answer, so I went in and—well, there she was on the floor. It took me a moment to realize she was dead. Just lying there dead. Quite peacefully dead. It was a fearful shock, the sort of thing you don't believe can happen. I'd come all that way just to talk to her and I was too late. It didn't make any sense at all. It still doesn't.'

'I suppose you didn't know she'd had a severe stroke two years ago,' Nigel said. 'Or did you?'

The man shook his head. 'No, I knew nothing about it.'

'It didn't happen to occur to you that you were still married to her and might be able to squeeze some money out of her? Since she'd connived at your bigamy you had some sort of hold on her.'

Halliday again shook his head. 'I don't happen to be in need of money. I'm reasonably prosperous. I'm a director in the firm of Robins, Halliday, Calthorpe, based in Liverpool. Import and export. And what difference would it have made if I'd known that she'd had a stroke?'

'None, I suppose, unless you thought that if she was a very sick woman, not quite herself, you might be able to frighten her into doing something for you. But I agree it isn't likely. Forget it. What did you do when you found her?'

'Nothing for a few minutes,' Halliday replied. 'Then it struck me that there was a very unpleasant smell in the room as if something was burning, and I thought that perhaps Annabel had left something cooking somewhere before she had that stroke that killed her and that it might be going to set things on fire. So I went looking for the kitchen and found that—that woman, whoever she was, sitting at the table, obviously shot in the head. And then I remembered the gun that I'd seen lying beside Annabel on the floor in the other room. I hadn't paid any attention to it for some reason when I first saw it, it had just seemed part of the fantastic scene in there without any particular meaning. But of course it meant something to me after finding the other woman. It meant that Annabel had killed her, didn't it? Who was she? A housekeeper?'

'She was Annabel's younger sister, Caroline,' Nigel said.

'Caroline?' the man said thoughtfully. 'Of course, I remember Caroline. A baby, or only two or three years old when Annabel and I got married. She was being taken care of by some aunt of theirs. So Annabel killed her sister, did she?'

'It isn't impossible that she did,' Nigel said. 'But you didn't turn off the stove, you left it to burn.'

'Yes, that's when I was a complete fool,' Halliday replied. 'I simply panicked. I wanted to get away as fast as I could. I rushed out of the house, got in my car and drove off. I believe I saw you—' he looked at Gavin—'standing in the doorway of that cottage across the way.'

Gavin nodded. 'When you remembered the gun, did you by any chance handle it?'

Another lurid flash of lightning lit up the room, as closely followed as before by thunder.

'No, I didn't touch the gun,' Halliday said.

'I don't believe him' Barbara said abruptly. 'It wouldn't be natural in the circumstances not to have picked it up and looked at it. Then of course he'd have realized his fingerprints would be on it, so he'd have cleaned it up with his handkerchief and put it back where he found it . . . That's to say, if he really did find it beside Annabel. He might have found it beside Caroline, who'd just used it to kill herself.'

'No, Caroline didn't kill herself,' Helena said. 'I know she didn't.'

'How d'you know?' Barbara asked.

'Don't ask me that, I just do,' Helena said. 'There's been murder in this house, not suicide.'

'Rubbish,' Barbara said. 'You don't know a thing about it.'

'She just could be right by chance, all the same,' Nigel said, 'though I can't think why Mr Halliday should have moved the gun. Now I think we'd better phone the police.'

'I swear to you I never touched the gun,' Halliday said.

'It isn't for us to try to settle that,' Nigel said. 'It's the police you'll have to convince, though they aren't going to thank us for bringing them out in this weather.'

He left the room.

'Caroline,' Halliday said again. 'I remember now, I once read something about her in some article about Annabel. I always used to pay attention to those when I saw one. She was an actress, wasn't she?'

'So you'd never seen her since she was an infant,' Barbara said sceptically. 'Are you sure it wasn't really her you came here to see?'

'Why ever should I do that?' Halliday asked.

'Oh, you might have had a reason. She was a very attractive woman.'

'I tell you I didn't know her, I didn't recognize her when I saw her dead, I thought she was the housekeeper.'

'Tell that to the police,' Barbara said in the tone that she might have used if she had been advising him to tell it to the Marines.

As lightning blazed again Nigel came back into the room. 'They'll soon be here,' he said.

They were there in about twenty minutes, Frost, Crewe and a third man, as if they felt that the man whom they had come to fetch might be violent and that it might be useful to be sure that there were enough of them to restrain him. The storm had abated a little by then. The claps of thunder were farther apart and not quite so loud and the rain had lessened. The three men hurried into the house and were introduced to Jerome Halliday, who had stood up on hearing them come in and stood patiently waiting to be told what they wanted to do with him.

This was simply to take him to the police station in Tolcaster. Frost told him that he could have a solicitor present when they interviewed him and that he was not compelled to answer their questions, but he gave an indifferent shrug of his shoulders and said that he was quite prepared to make a statement without any legal guidance, anyway for the present. What he might want later, he implied, depended on what happened in the police station. When it came to the point, he might make up his mind not to talk at all. If that meant that he might have to spend the night in a police cell, he had no doubt seen worse places in his time. He left with Frost and Crewe, the third man having been brought, it appeared, to drive the Mercedes away on the tail of the police car. The rain had given its glossy grey a gleaming polish and as it circled the soaked gravel of the courtyard its wheels sent up a spray of water.

'I'd like another drink,' Helena said as Nigel closed the front door after the cars had gone.

'You've just had one,' Barbara said.

'One of the best reasons for having another,' Helena

asserted. 'Anyway, I need one. I found it a terrible strain, listening to that man. I always find it very difficult to pretend. I'm normally completely open with everybody. And pretending one believed his story! What a story! What will happen to him? Will they charge him with the murder this evening?'

'Suppose his story's true,' Nigel said as he brought her a drink.

'But we know no one else could have done it,' Helena said. 'None of us really believes that Annabel murdered her sister and if anyone else besides that man had come into the house, Gavin would have seen him, we're agreed on that, aren't we?'

'Not exactly,' Gavin said. 'Whoever it was would probably have been afraid I might see him, unless, like Halliday, he didn't know I was there. But the fact is that all the time Leslie Jay was with me I had my back to the window, then when she left I picked up *The Times* and had a go at the crossword, so I wasn't watching what was happening outside. And after that you telephoned, so again I wasn't looking out.'

'Coincidence,' Helena said. 'I told you, I don't like coincidences. If you can understand them you can see they were meant to happen. But now tell me about Barbara turning this place into a guest-house. Is she going to buy it from you, Nigel?'

'I don't believe that's exactly her idea,' he answered. 'As I told you, she seems to think that if I let her run it as a guest-house I'll find it an excellent investment.'

'So you will,' Barbara said. 'Once the word gets round of how good the food is—'

'But you don't know the first thing about handling people,' Helena interrupted. 'You never have. And that's the most important thing in a project like that. To be able to be friendly with people, to make them feel welcome, that comes first. And you know you've never had a trace of tact or understanding of other people's peculiar needs. Everyone's different and you need to be sensitive about it and not just rely on filling them up with your precious salads and what not. I've nothing against salads, indeed I like them very much, but I think there's more to human relationships than what you put into your stomachs.'

'Human relationships, as you call them, can't flourish on a lot of upset digestions,' Barbara said. 'I believe they've destroyed more friendships, perhaps even marriages, than most of us like to admit. I know my own digestion has sometimes interfered disastrously when I had important decisions to take.'

'Of course, I might be able to help you,' Helena said.

'Help me?' Barbara said. 'You? What do you mean?'

'I was just thinking that if we pooled our resources, with you looking after the practical side of the business, because I must admit I've no understanding of that kind of thing, and with me handling the people, it would be a very interesting experiment. I know you don't believe it, but I've often helped people who desperately needed it. I can't tell you how I do it, it's just a power I seem to have, and I have to use it sparingly, because it doesn't always work—'

'I'll bet it doesn't!' Barbara broke in.

'You wouldn't say that if you'd seen some of the letters I've had, thanking me,' Helena said. 'Nigel, what do you think? Don't you think it would be wonderfully worth trying?'

'I think it's time we got supper,' Nigel replied.

'But seriously,' Helena said, 'I've always longed for an opportunity to organize the way I can help people. At present it's just a case of word getting around among people who happen to meet one another, but if they were to hear there was somewhere where they could have a really perfect rest, here at the foot of these beautiful downs, and of course with good food—'

'Thank you!' Barbara said.

'And with a special atmosphere where they could feel really at peace, don't you think, since one has to remember such things, that it really might be a good investment?'

'What I think is that you and Barbara would murder each other in a week,' Nigel said, 'and this house has seen enough of murder. Now what about supper?'

'I'll see to it,' Barbara said and departed to the kitchen.

They had omelettes, made from the eggs that Barbara had brought with her, and salad and some of the plums that she had brought. Later, after some more discussion, it was settled in an only mildly acrimonious way that Gavin's suggestion should be adopted and that he should bring his belongings over from the cottage and that the two women should sleep there. The rain had almost ceased by then and the lightning was only an occasional pale flash, flickering in the approaching darkness. What Nigel would eventually do with the house was not discussed any more.

At the thought of having to spend the evening together both sisters had retreated into what was nearly silence, sullen and hostile, but they went over to the cottage with Gavin and when he left them to return to the house were arguing about nothing more dangerous than which bedroom each should have. Nigel took Gavin up to the spare bedroom on the first floor and helped him to make up the bed, then said that he was going to have another drink, then go to bed himself. With a groan he said that he had never felt so tired in his life. Gavin stayed downstairs for only a little while after Nigel had gone up to his room, then went up again to his.

It was a pleasant room, bigger than the one that he had had in the cottage and the bed was wider and more comfortable, but sleep did not come to him. A weary rest-lessness possessed him and continued until he realized that a good deal of the tension that was keeping him wide awake came from the fact that he was shrinking from thinking about Caroline. Not only Caroline dead, but Caroline alive. What had she meant to him?

He had not meant much to her, he was sure of that. But was he failing her in some way by not feeling far more pain-ful grief than he did? He felt shock, horror and a great rage against a figure that stayed shadowy in his imagination, but of true grief, in the sense of a deep and irreparable loss, he seemed not to feel a great deal. Perhaps that would come later when shock itself had had a chance to lessen. But now he even found some difficulty in remembering her face very clearly.

That was partly because the image of her sitting col-lapsed over her cookery book in the kitchen overlay the one of her that had been with him for so long, vital and beauti-ful and full of dazzling energy. But, trying to be honest with himself, he admitted that it was partly because in all the time that they had been separated he had not really thought of her so very often.

But that shadowy figure must be found. He was begin-ning to be fairly sure who it was, except that it seemed im-possible. But there must be some explanation, something that he had failed to understand. Struggling with the prob-lem of it with more concentration than he was really cap-able of in his nervously exhausted state, he drifted off into dream-haunted sleep.

A clap of thunder woke him, or what in his dream and while he was only slowly returning to consciousness he be-lieved to have been thunder. But the night was still. No rain drummed on the window of his bedroom. The patch of sky that he could see through it looked cloudless, with even a few stars shining in the dark expanse. And suddenly he knew that it had not been thunder that he had heard, or even anything very like it. Scrambling out of bed, he ran to Nigel's room.

He was lying on one of the beds in the room that he had shared with Annabel, still and white except for the great patch of red that covered his chest. He was breathing, though only in short, irregular gasps. Somewhere in the house Gavin heard a door slam. For an instant it seemed to him that that was what must come before anything else. Before anything else, he must find out who had been here, who had fired the shot that had wakened him. But Nigel had given a faint moan, as if he were trying to say something, and Gavin stayed, dropping on his knees beside the bed.

The bedclothes were thrown back, as if Nigel had been trying to get up when the shot had hit him and one arm dangled over the edge of the bed. Gavin caught at the hand that hung there. It lay limp and unresponsive in his, then he thought that he felt it contract slightly and he tried to find the pulse. Where Nigel's heart should have been beating there was only a thick puddle of blood that seemed to be steadily growing.

Nigel murmured something. Gavin leant over him, bringing his ear close to Nigel's lips.

'My fault,' Nigel whispered. 'Didn't do it, but my fault.'

'Nigel, I'm going to call an ambulance.' There was a telephone by the bed and Gavin let go of Nigel's hand, dialling rapidly 999. Then when the call had been answered he picked up the limp hand again, feeling for that contraction which had told him that there was still a trace of life left in his brother. But it was motionless now.

'The house,' Nigel managed to go on whispering, though it was difficult for Gavin to make out what he was saying. 'If the girls want it, try to see they get it . . . Thicker than water . . . And Gavin . . .'

'Don't try to talk,' Gavin said. 'The ambulance will soon be here.'

'No good . . . My fault, that's why I said nothing . . .'

He gave a little groan. He was dead by the time that the ambulance arrived.

CHAPTER 9

But before the ambulance came several things had happened.

Gavin had tried to telephone Desmond Jay. He was aware that this was almost certainly futile, as Nigel, he was sure, was beyond being helped by any doctor on earth. Yet if a doctor could be brought to him, it seemed that it ought to be done. The telephone in the Jays' house rang a number of times before at last it was picked up and Marion's voice said, 'Dr Jay's house.'

The time was a quarter to three.

'Marion, this is Gavin,' he said. 'Is your husband there?'

'I'm sorry, he was called out on an emergency about half an hour ago,' she answered. 'What is it, Gavin?' Her tone was level but anxious. 'Can I do anything?'

'I don't think anyone can,' he said. 'It's Nigel. Someone got in and—' His voice dried up to a croak. He had to clear his throat before he could go on. When he did he spoke harshly and curtly. 'Someone got into the house and shot him. I think he's dead, but if your husband could have come—'

'Oh, Gavin, I'm so sorry!' she broke in. She sounded breathless. 'Where are you? In the cottage?'

'No, in the house. I stayed here tonight. The girls are in the cottage. I heard the shot, but by the time I got to his room whoever came had got away. I've rung for an ambulance.'

'Girls?' she said. 'What girls? Oh, your sister Barbara. But I thought you'd stayed with her in the cottage.'

'My sister Helena arrived in the afternoon, so I left the cottage to them. I haven't told them yet what's happened. I'll ring off now and do that.'

'Wait a moment. I'm so sorry Desmond can't come to you, but I'll come. Perhaps there's nothing anyone can do, but I used to be a nurse. I'll be round in a few minutes.'

He was not sure that he wanted her, but did not think of arguing. Putting the telephone down, he dialled the cottage. He had to wait for an answer for even longer than he had when he telephoned the Jays, but he held on, letting the ringing continue relentlessly until at last Barbara's sleepy voice said, 'Yes?'

'Get ready for some very bad news, Barbara,' he said. He was in better control of himself than he had been when he first spoke to Marion. 'You and Helena had better get over here as quickly as you can.'

'What, at this hour?' she demanded incredulously.

'Yes, at once. I'm just going to call the police and I think you'd better be here when they arrive. Someone got into the house and shot Nigel. I was asleep, but the noise of the shot woke me. I've rung for an ambulance, though I think it's already too late to help.'

'Shot Nigel? Killed him, d'you mean? He's dead?' The questions came in jerks.

'I think so,' Gavin said. 'He said just a few words to me when I found him, then I think that was the end.'

'Who did it?' She sounded now strangely like her usual brusque self. It was probably how she would have sounded whatever he had had to tell her.

'They got away while I was with Nigel,' Gavin answered. 'I had to stay with him.'

'I see. Well, we'll be over at once.'

She put the telephone down even before he did.

After that he telephoned the police. To track down Detective-Inspector Frost was the most complicated thing that he had had to do that evening. The unfortunate man had gone home to have a little sleep and it seemed to Gavin that someone else might have been sent in his place if that would hasten matters, and someone, he was assured, would come, but plainly Frost had to be found and informed of what had happened. After that Gavin went back to his bedroom, shed his pyjamas and got into a shirt, trousers and slippers, then thoughtfully went downstairs again.

He went into the dining-room. As he was expecting, the window was wide open. It was through the window, broken by Annabel's wild shot on the Friday evening, that the intruder had got into the house. Whoever had come in had been able to put a hand in through the gaping hole in the glass, undo the latch, push the window open and climb into the room. Not, however, without leaving tracks, for under the window was the remains of the puddle that had been made by the rain in the afternoon, and footsteps, a little muddy, led from the window to the door, across the hall and to the bottom of the stairs. There, after the first few steps, they faded, as the carpet soaked up the damp that had been on somebody's shoes. Not very large shoes, Gavin was inclined to think. It seemed to him that they had probably been made by someone wearing Wellington boots, for they had the blurred sort of outlines that these might have made, but it was difficult to be sure how large they were. He was contemplating them when the door-knocker sounded and he found Barbara and Helena outside.

They had not bothered to dress, but were in their dressing-gowns, and the moment that they stepped inside their slippers made damp marks, obliterating those that had been left crossing the hall by the murderer. Gavin had not been prepared for this and was too slow to stop them. He realized that the courtyard was still sodden from the heavy rain that had fallen during the storm, so of course their slippers were wet. But he stoppped them going into the dining-room. The tracks there could be protected.

'Where is he?' Barbara asked.

'In his room,' Gavin said.

'Upstairs?'

'Yes.'

'Oh God, oh God!' Helena whimpered. 'You're quite sure, are you, he's dead? Oh, this house! I told you, it's evil.'

'Can't you shut up?' Barbara snarled and went pounding up the staircase.

The muddy prints of her slippers, followed closely by Helena's, showed clearly almost to the top. The two women disappeared into Nigel's room, the door of which stood open. Gavin hesitated, then followed them up.

He found them standing in silence on either side of Nigel's bed. He lay with one arm dangling over the edge of it, as Gavin had left it. His face was the yellowish grey of death, with the red stain on his chest already beginning to darken a little. Both women were very pale and for the first time that he could remember Gavin thought that he could detect in their stricken faces, which were really so different, some strange trace of a resemblance. There was even a resemblance too, he thought, though he was aware that this might be imaginary, to the handsome face on the pillow. And for all he knew, it was also to be seen on his own. They were all one family, Cleavers who tended to avoid one another when they could, but who now, with their elder brother leaving them entirely, were brought dreadfully together.

Tears began to trickle slowly down Helena's cheeks and she made a sudden dash for the door. Barbara stood rigidly still, then made a curious choking sound which might have been the beginning of a sob and followed her. Gavin stayed where he was, looking all round the room as if there might be something there that would tell him something, but there was nothing. Slowly he went after his sisters and found them in the drawing-room, sitting side by side on the sofa where Gavin remembered Marion sitting beside Annabel, telling her how wonderful her books were. Both books had been written by the dead man upstairs. Surprisingly, Helena had her arm round Barbara's shoulders, as if to comfort her. Tears were still quietly running down Helena's cheeks, but Barbara's gaunt body was shaking. As Gavin came into the room Helena dropped her arm and fumbled for a handkerchief in the pocket of her dressing-gown.

Barbara rubbed a hand across her forehead, making an effort to steady herself.

'You said on the telephone he got away without you seeing him,' she said.

'Yes, I was with Nigel,' Gavin answered. 'I heard a door close down here and I almost ran down, but Nigel was trying to speak to me and that seemed more important than seeing who it was.'

'Yes, of course. Did he actually manage to say anything?'

'Yes, he said he wanted you to have the house, if you wanted it.'

'The house?' she said, sounding puzzled. 'Oh, this house. That absurd idea of mine. He was worrying about that at the end, was he? That feels terrible.'

'You don't want it?' Gavin said.

'Of course not. That was all just talk. Didn't he say anything else?'

'He said something was his fault and that was why he'd said nothing. I think he meant the murder of Caroline.'

'But he didn't say he'd done it? He didn't meant that?'

'Of course he didn't!' Helena cried. 'Didn't I tell you he couldn't have? And now we know for certain he didn't. But it wasn't Annabel either. She wasn't here tonight, was she? And Caroline didn't kill herself, because she couldn't have dropped the gun beside Annabel after she was dead. No, someone got in here that morning, whatever that Jay girl says about not having seen anyone, and it wasn't Jerome Halliday, because the police have got him, haven't they? Or d'you think they'd have let him go?'

'I shouldn't think so,' Gavin said. 'But it rather looks to me as if someone got in here tonight who didn't know I was in the house. Someone, that's to say, who didn't know you'd come, Helena, and that you and Barbara would be in the cottage while I'd moved in here. They didn't know there'd be any hurry about getting away until they heard me move in my room. They might even have thought they could stay to clean up their footprints. But we can't be sure it was the person who killed Caroline.'

'What do you think Nigel meant when he said that was his fault and that was why he hadn't talked?' Barbara asked. 'That sounds strange to me.'

'I've no idea, you know,' Gavin said, 'though I don't see how it's possible.'

'Of course that girl Leslie lied,' Helena said. 'She did see someone come in. The question is, whom would she lie for?'

Barbara stood up abruptly. 'There's someone outside,' she said. 'Who is it. Is it the police?'

But it was Marion and Leslie Jay.

The first thing that Gavin noticed about them as they stepped into the hall was that they were both wearing Wellingtons. They were also wearing trousers and rain-coats. Like those of Barbara and Helena, the footprints that they left on the floor were muddy, but except that he was careful to keep the door of the dining-room closed so that the new prints would not mask those that had been left behind

there, Gavin did not trouble to preserve those in the hall or
on the staircase.

When Marion asked him with a curiously professional
air of calm, which reminded him of what she had said about
once having been a nurse, where Nigel was, he gestured at
the staircase and she and Leslie went quickly up to Nigel's
room. Gavin felt that he had to follow them, though he was
not sure why, since there was nothing there that they could
do either to help or that ought to be prevented, and he
found them standing side by side just inside the door, saying nothing. When he came into the room behind them
Marion turned, laid a hand for a moment on his arm, then
went downstairs. Leslie gave him a strange, long look, then
went after her mother.

This time Gavin lingered for a little while, alone with
Nigel. He was thinking of what Helena had said about Leslie having lied about not having seen anyone go into the
house before Caroline was killed, and also of the question
that she had asked: For whom would Leslie lie? For her
mother or her father? Probably. For herself? Yes, certainly.
But the trouble was that all three of them had known that
he was staying in the cottage and to have walked in boldly
to commit murder when he might have been at his window
would have been taking an insane risk. It had been by mere
chance that he had not been looking out. However, none of
them had known of Helena's arrival and if one of them had
come to the house that night, whichever it was would not
have known that there was much risk in coming. It was the
blatancy with which the risk had been taken the first time
that baffled him. He stood gazing almost unseeingly at
Nigel, sure that he at least had known who the murderer
was and that more than once he had almost told Gavin
what he knew, but then had deliberately held the knowledge back because he felt that the guilt was at least partly
his. And that told Gavin a good deal, even if Nigel had not

intended that it should. But it did not answer the question of how anyone could have been mad enough to walk into a house in broad daylight to commit a murder when that person knew that there would almost certainly be an audience.

Gavin gave a sigh and went slowly downstairs again.

As he went into the drawing-room, where the four women were, all standing in a group, he heard Barbara say harshly, 'Where did the gun that killed Nigel come from?'

No one answered.

She went on, 'The gun that killed Caroline was the one that Annabel said she had had for years and which she showed to you all on the Friday evening. But the police have got that now. So where did the one that killed Nigel come from?'

'All sorts of people have guns, haven't they?' Marion said hesitantly. 'Guns the police know nothing about.'

'I expect Oliver Penbury has a few,' Gavin said. 'He belongs to a gun club, doesn't he? But perhaps his are licensed.'

There was another silence, then Leslie turned on him a stare rather like the one that she had given him upstairs.

'You must be crazy,' she said after a moment.

'I've wondered about that sometimes myself,' Gavin said. 'I've occasionally caught myself teetering on what seemed to be the edge of sheer insanity. I imagine most people have, even if they weren't exactly aware of it.'

'But you're suggesting that Oliver might have murdered Nigel!' Leslie said fiercely.

'Oh no, I didn't mean to give that impression,' Gavin said. 'I only observed that I thought he might have some guns. I seem to remember you talking about some club he belongs to after Annabel had done her shooting and nobody knew what to do about picking up the gun. But it's a fact, isn't it, that he didn't know I was staying at the cottage and he just might have walked in here, assuming the cottage was empty.'

'But he happens to have an alibi,' Leslie declared.

'Of course he does,' Marion said. 'When you came to us, Gavin, after finding Annabel and Caroline dead, I rang up the surgery at once to ask Oliver to get out here, and he was there.'

'And I expect he's got an alibi now,' Leslie said. 'He's certainly at home. I'll telephone his lodgings if you like and you can be sure he'll answer.'

'No, don't do that,' Gavin said. 'I'm sure he needs his sleep. I know I'm not talking rationally. I'm just thinking of—oh, all sorts of possibilities, and impossibilities too.'

'Anyway, what would be his motive for murdering Caroline?' Helena asked. 'Was he in love with her too? I thought it was Nigel who was.'

The answer to this was unexpected. Marion suddenly broke down into a storm of weeping. It began with a thin, high wail, then changed to choking sobs, and dropping into a chair, she rocked her body to and fro with her hands over her face, her shoulders shaking.

Leslie stood looking at her for a moment without moving and with a trace of what Gavin thought was contempt on her face, then she sat down on the arm of the chair and put an arm round her mother.

'Don't,' she said. 'Please don't.'

Marion seemed to shudder away from her daughter's embrace, but the sobs grew quieter.

'I know what the trouble is,' Leslie said. 'You've been afraid from the beginning that Father did it, haven't you? You've actually believed he came here and killed her so that no one else could have her. After all, you didn't know where he was that morning. And you don't know where he is now. That emergency on which he was called out, you don't know anything about it, do you? And he might have got hold of one of Oliver's guns, I suppose. But you're quite wrong, Mother dear. If he'd come in yesterday morning, when I was with Gavin in the cottage, I'd have seen him, wouldn't I? And I didn't.' Her tone became more insistent. 'I didn't, Mother. You've been wrong about everything.'

Marion dropped her hands and although the tears were still streaming down her face, she said, 'You really didn't?'

'No.'

They gazed into one another's eyes.

'You didn't see anyone?' Marion said.

'No one.'

'You're quite sure?'

'Absolutely sure.'

Gavin found himself looking as if he were hypnotized at the Wellington boots that both women were wearing. As much to detach himself from this as anything, he turned to Helena.

'Why did you say you thought Nigel was in love with Caroline?' he asked.

'Well, wasn't he?' she said.

'He never told me so.'

She gave an impatient sigh. 'I don't suppose he would. But wasn't it why she stayed on here? There must have been some reason for that.'

'Of course there was,' Barbara said. 'Helena's right, I believe. It explains a lot of things.'

It was so unusual to hear the two sisters agreeing with one another about anything that Gavin did not know how to reply, and in the silence that followed, broken only by Marion's sniffing as she brought her tears under control, the door-knocker sounded. Detective-Inspector Frost with Detective-Constable Crewe had arrived.

Frost had the angry look of a man who feels he is being deprived of sleep to which he has a right. Crewe had his usual slightly shabby air of untidiness, and looked merely casual as he normally did and no more disturbed at being called out at that hour of the morning than he would have at any other time of the day or night. Perhaps being much the younger of the two men he was the more adaptable. Frost demanded where the shooting of Mr Cleaver had occurred and as Gavin gestured towards Nigel's room, Frost started towards the stairs. But at the bottom of them he stood still.

'Who's the fool who's been going up and down these stairs?' he demanded in sharp exasperation. 'Look at them—a bloody mass of muddy footprints! Who's been up and down?'

'We all have,' Gavin said.

'Just to help matters, eh?' Frost said. 'Many thanks. Just what we needed! But you're in slippers yourself. You didn't make any of those prints.'

'I suppose I didn't,' Gavin agreed.

'But why didn't you stop the rest of them who came in from outside with mud on their shoes going running up?' Frost said, looking round. 'It's good and muddy outside after the storm. Didn't any of you think of taking your shoes off before you went charging up the stairs, or weren't there any footprints there when you came? It won't be much good now trying to trace who may have made which, but didn't any of you see anything?'

'I'm sorry,' Barbara said. 'I didn't myself, and I agree we were at fault, but I don't think you can blame my brother for not stopping us before we'd done irreparable damage to what may have been valuable clues. Like the rest of us, he was in a state of shock.'

'Yes, yes. Well, we'll talk about that later,' Frost said. 'Come on, Bob.'

He and Crewe went up the stairs.

When they came downstairs again Frost did a good deal of telephoning. This would mean, Gavin realized, that soon other men would be coming, as they had the day before. An ambulance arrived before any of them and the driver was told to wait. Gavin and the four women waited in the drawing-room, silent now as if they were all listening for what might be going forward in the house.

After a while, before his team of assistants had arrived, Frost looked in on them and said, 'Mr Cleaver, I'd like a word with you.'

Crewe, it appeared, had remained upstairs.

Gavin had been standing by the door on to the terrace, looking out into the darkness of the starlit night. There was not yet any sign of dawn in the sky. He walked out into the hall, but when Frost was about to enter the dining-room for the talk that he wanted, Gavin stopped him.

'Wait a moment,' he said. 'There's something I want to show you.'

He passed Frost to the door of the dining-room and opened it.

'I know I didn't manage to stop the footprints in the hall and on the stairs getting messed up,' he said, 'but what about these?'

He pointed to the prints that led from what was left of the puddle under the window to the door.

'I see,' Frost said, carefully avoiding them as he went forward into the room. 'Yes, they may mean something.'

'Of course they mean something,' Gavin said, following him.

'But perhaps not what they seem to mean,' Frost said.

'I don't understand,' Gavin said. 'Aren't they the footprints of whoever murdered my brother?'

'That's what they look like.' There was an odd note of reluctance in Frost's voice.

'It's what they are, isn't it?' Gavin insisted.

'Quite right, anyway, to have seen they didn't get messed up like the others. Mr Cleaver, you were spending the night

here, alone with your brother, I understand. Just why was
that? Why didn't you remain in the cottage over the way?'

Dodging the footprints, they had both walked to the far
end of the room and sat down at the table.

'It seemed the easiest way to arrange things,' Gavin said.
'My sister Barbara had arrived in the morning and settled
in there with me, then my other sister, Helena, turned up
here in the afternoon and my brother suggested she should
sleep in the spare room here, but she was obviously scared
of the idea. She didn't like the feeling of sleeping in a house
where there'd been a murder. So I moved over so that the
two of them could sleep in the cottage.'

'Were you expecting this second sister?' Frost asked.

His manner was more abrasive than Gavin had yet found
it and there was a look in the wide-spaced eyes in the big
man's broad, ruddy face which struck him as a kind of
smouldering anger. Perhaps it was only the look of someone
deprived of sleep when he happened to need it badly,
but it gave Gavin a feeling of dismay that was almost
fear.

'Not really,' he said. 'She'd rung up the day before and
suggested that she might come here, but I did my best to
put her off. I wasn't sure then that I'd be staying myself.'

'But she came all the same.'

'Yes.'

'Suppose she hadn't.'

'Well?'

'If she hadn't, Mr Cleaver, would you have remained in
the cottage, or would you have found some reason for sleeping here?'

Gavin began to think he understood what was in the
other man's mind.

'I'd have stayed in the cottage,' he said. 'And if what
you're saying is that as I was alone here in the house with
my brother, I'd the best opportunity to kill him, what do

you make of those footprints? Aren't they a woman's?'

'They look like it, I admit,' Frost said.

'Then why do you think they may not be?'

'It's only that I like to think of all possibilities,' Frost said wearily. 'I'm sorry if I seem unreasonable to you. I'm never very reasonable at this time of the night. It's only that you had all the time you could have needed to fake them somehow, if you should have had that in mind. There are women's shoes in the house, aren't there? Mrs Cleaver's and Miss Astor's. I don't know if possibly you could have squeezed your feet into a pair of them to take just a few steps, but it's something we'll have to look into. It seems to me a bit strange that just these prints have been so carefully preserved when the ones there might have been in the hall and on the stairs have been trampled over. I can't help wondering if there were really ever any prints out there at all till your visitors got here.'

Gavin felt his temper beginning to rise. It was a feeling that was unusual to him, even when handling the most troublesome boys in a class that he was trying to make interesting, and he was rather afraid of it. Though his face grew white, which was something of which he was not aware, his voice grew even quieter and colder than it normally was.

'If you're suggesting that I murdered my brother,' he said, 'will you tell me what I've done with the shoes I borrowed, and when I got hold of a gun?'

'Those are questions that may be answered in time,' Frost said. 'Certainly not at the moment. Don't get me wrong, Mr Cleaver, I'm not accusing you of anything. I'm only doing that good old act of exploring avenues. If I happen to believe that sooner or later we'll find those shoes, well, I could be wrong. I can't tell you how often I've been wrong in the cases I've handled, though in the end I sometimes get them right.'

'This avenue you're exploring is a dead end,' Gavin said frigidly.

'No doubt, no doubt,' Frost said. 'But I can't help thinking there's something very odd about the fact that a murderer walked into this house in broad daylight yesterday and shot Miss Astor when he or she almost certainly knew that you could have seen whoever it was, and yet apparently you didn't. Or you say you didn't. And then you're alone here in the house with your brother when he's murdered, and there are a few clear little footprints in here to show that some small-footed person came in through the window, when you of course were inside. But you'd plenty of time, hadn't you, with both your sisters in the cottage and no one here to see what you were doing, to arrange the scene? And then, of course, there's the motive.'

'Oddly enough, that's just what I was going to ask you about,' Gavin said. 'I admit that nothing you've said is actually nonsense. I can see that from your point of view it may make a kind of sense. But unless you assume that I'm out of my mind, which perhaps you do, and you must have had contact with far more people who are than I ever have, will you tell me why I should have killed either of those people, for both of whom I actually had a good deal of affection?'

Frost wiped a large hand over his face as if he were deliberately erasing all expression from it.

'Do you know that your brother and Caroline Astor were married in Oxford a fortnight ago?' he asked.

Gavin said nothing.

Still expressionless, Frost said, 'You aren't surprised.'

What surprised Gavin was that he should feel as little surprise as he did. It was almost as if he had been expecting it.

'Did you know about it?' Frost asked.

Gavin was slow to reply, but then he said, 'No, but it

explains a number of things. First of all why Caroline Astor stayed on here and gave up her profession when she was just becoming a success in it. That's puzzled everybody. But if she and my brother were enough in love, it isn't really a problem, is it? I didn't believe they were at first because he confessed to me he'd been having an affair with another woman, and who that was is fairly obvious, isn't it? Then there's the slightly curious matter of my sister-in-law's will. Caroline persuaded her to sign it by letting her think it was just another contract for a book, yet she cut herself out of it when she could easily have given herself some substantial legacy. But if she'd married, or been just about to marry my brother, it was just common sense to do that. Money left directly to her would have been quite heavily taxed, but if it all went to my brother as Annabel's husband, there'd have been no tax to pay at all.'

'Except that he and Mrs Cleaver in fact weren't married,' Frost pointed out.

'But if there hadn't been a murder that probably wouldn't have come out, would it?' Gavin said. 'He and Annabel had been accepted as a married couple for twenty years. He told me himself that he'd intended to claim that that was what they'd been whenever she died. He and Caroline both knew that it wasn't going to be long before that happened. Annabel was a very sick woman.'

'Strange that he should have troubled about marrying Miss Astor when he was accustomed, as you might say, to getting on without it.'

'I dare say she insisted on it. She may have realized that he wasn't perhaps an altogether trustworthy person.'

The fact that he plainly had not been still gave Gavin a stinging pain when he thought of it. He had been deluded by Nigel in so many ways for so many years.

'Incidentally, my brother was particularly keen that I should come here this summer,' he went on. 'That wasn't customary, but I think there were two reasons for it. One was simply that he wanted me to occupy the cottage to make it quite clear to that other woman I mentioned that the affair was over and that their usual meeting-place wasn't available. The other, I believe now, after what you've told me, was that he wanted to let me know about the marriage. He knew there'd been a time when Caroline meant a great deal to me and I don't think he'd have wanted me to go on deluding myself that perhaps, after all, she still cared for me.'

'And weren't you saying just now that you'd no motive for killing Miss Astor?' Frost said. 'Jealousy's one of the commonest causes of murder.'

'My brother hadn't yet told me about his marriage when Caroline was murdered.'

'How do I know if that's true?'

'I suppose I've just got to hope that you'll come round to believing me, as I hope you'll believe I didn't see anyone walk into the house to murder her, or walk in to do it myself. And that I didn't arrange for my sisters to sleep in the cottage, so that I'd be here alone with my brother and able to take my revenge on him. And that I didn't make these footprints.'

He gestured at the muddy prints, dry now, that led from the window to the door.

Frost gave them another look, then nodded absently.

'All you say may be true, Mr Cleaver,' he said, 'but there's a certain point which I'm a bit surprised you haven't raised yourself. I believe you went for a long walk on the downs on the Saturday morning.'

'Yes,' Gavin said.

'And got home about half past eleven, isn't that right?'

'I believe so.'

'So perhaps whoever came into the house came in before then. It would have had to be someone whom Mrs Cleaver and Miss Astor knew quite well, because didn't Miss Astor answer the telephone when your sister rang up to ask for your number, at what we know was only a very short time before Miss Astor was shot? So that means, you see, that if this hypothetical visitor I'm talking about did come in before you got home, he was here for quite a while. And it could have been that he saw you get home and so knew that you hadn't seen him arrive and that it was safe for him to commit murder.'

'But how could he have expected to get away?' Gavin asked. 'He couldn't have known that both Jerome Halliday and I would be coming to the house, and that we'd both leave it in a hurry.'

'You don't think much of my suggestion, then,' Frost said. 'You'd sooner I went on being rather suspicious of you.'

'I assume the person you're talking about is Dr Jay,' Gavin said. 'Some people seem to have an idea that he'd fallen in love with Caroline and been rejected. The jealousy motive that you like. And he was out that morning, making calls on his patients. You'd have to check up whom he actually did see. And he might have called on Annabel and stayed chatting with her for a time. And of course he knew where the gun was, and for tonight's killing he might have been able to steal a gun from Dr Penbury, a friend of his and probably to be his son-in-law. It all very nearly fits. There's just one thing that doesn't.'

'Those footprints?'

'Actually I was thinking of something else. Where was Annabel while he was helping himself to the gun from the bureau and committing murder? You know, my brother rather wanted her to be proved the murderer. He felt that it couldn't do her any harm and that she couldn't harm anyone else. I remember he used the phrase, there's no danger from the dead. And for some reason I disagreed with him, I don't know why, but I had a strange feeling that Annabel was dangerous. Absurd, of course. He thought he knew who the murderer was and he wanted to cover up for her. That was almost the last thing he said.'

'Which suggests Miss Jay, of course.'

'How do you know about that?'

'Bob Crewe's been talking in the village, and he got it out of Mrs Nevin. She knew all about that affair and you might think that meant that half the village knew about it, but it happens she isn't a gossip. Bob told me it was hard work, getting her to talk about the family, but she did in the end. But the fact is, it doesn't help much.'

'Why not?'

Gavin was fairly sure of the reply and Frost said what he was expecting.

'Because of all people, having just been with you, she'd have known you could see her walk across the courtyard to the house. And having paid you that visit when she did, she couldn't have called on Mrs Cleaver while you were walking on the downs.'

'So you prefer the theory that her father might have done it.'

'Didn't I call that a hypothesis?'

'And your suspicions of me—are they hypothetical too?'

For a moment Frost made no response, then he stood up.

'You may have another motive that we haven't talked about,' he said. 'If your brother died intestate, you and your sisters, as next of kin, stand to inherit a useful amount, if not quite a fortune once tax has been deducted and it's been split three ways, but still it's what I should definitely call useful. However, there are some people besides yourself that I want to question.'

He strode through to the drawing-room.

There were only three women in it.

CHAPTER 10

Leslie Jay had disappeared.

Marion was standing in the middle of the room, looking with fury at the two sisters who were sitting side by side on the sofa, both their faces sad, as if they were in sympathy with her in spite of what she was screaming at them.

'You devils!' she shrieked. 'You fiends! How did you dare say that?'

'I'm sorry,' Barbara said. 'We should perhaps have waited.'

'I'm very sorry,' Helena said. 'It's my fault, but I couldn't keep it in a moment longer. Poor girl, in spite of everything, I'm very sorry for what she must have suffered.'

'I'm not at all sorry for her,' Barbara said. 'She deserves everything she'll get. But I'm sorry for you, Mrs Jay, and for your poor husband.'

'Would you care to tell me what's been happening?' Frost said.

Marion turned to him, her face flushed and desperate.

'They've accused Leslie of having murdered Caroline and Nigel!' she screamed. 'They've got it all worked out and when they attacked her with it the poor girl lost her head and ran away. I don't know where she's gone. Perhaps home, or perhaps to Oliver.'

'Perhaps to London, to try to lose herself there, or even over the edge of some cliff, if she happens to know of a convenient one somewhere near,' Barbara said. 'I feel distinctly bad about it. I didn't expect her to react quite so violently, but I suppose I should have, since she must have been in an abnormal state of mind for some time to have done what she has.'

'Where's Crewe?' Frost asked abruptly.

'I think upstairs in my brother's room,' Barbara said, 'making sure none of us tampers with anything up there.'

'And the girl's gone?' Frost said. 'Will you tell me why, Mrs Jay?'

Marion dropped into a chair, as suddenly helpless as if she could not have stood up for a moment longer.

'I can't tell you,' she moaned. 'I can't bear it.'

He turned to the two women on the sofa.

'Will you explain?'

They both began at once. 'It's because she's the—'

Then they both stopped, looking at one another, as if each was waiting for the other to continue.

Then Barbara, as if accepting the responsibility of seniority, went on, 'We worked it out together last night. Neither of us felt like going to bed for a time, and we stayed up, talking the situation over. Of course it was obvious from the first that the girl had murdered Caroline. The only problem was how she'd dared to walk across the courtyard in broad daylight to commit a murder, when she knew better than anyone that my brother Gavin would probably see her.'

'And that he didn't was sheer coincidence,' Helena said. 'Only I don't believe in coincidences. They always make a pattern, if you can understand it.'

'Nonsense,' Barbara said. 'The girl couldn't have known that he was going to pick up *The Times* and start doing the crossword, and then that you'd telephone, and that he wouldn't be looking out of the window all that time.'

'I think she knew,' Helena said. 'Call it telepathy if you like, if you must give it a name, but at the back of her mind, without even knowing it, she knew. That's why she did what she did.'

'That's quite impossible. Sheer superstition.'

Even when they apparently agreed with one another on an important matter, the two sisters could not avoid arguing.

'If you'd tell me what you're talking about,' Frost said, 'it might help. What made Miss Jay walk across the courtyard to commit murder at a time when she was fairly sure she'd be seen?'

'She didn't,' Barbara said.

'No, of course she didn't,' Helena echoed her.

'Oh, I beg your pardon,' Frost said. 'I was under the impression that that was what you claimed she'd done.'

'Quite simply, when she walked over to the house,' Barbara said, 'she hadn't the least intention of committing murder, so of course she wasn't afraid to come.'

'Mind you, I don't exactly agree with that,' Helena said. 'I think murder had been in her mind for some time, it must have been, even if she wasn't conscious of it.'

'All right, I won't argue about that,' Barbara said, 'you may be right. But the fact is, when she walked over here after her talk with Gavin, she had no intention of committing any murder just then. She intended only to see if after all she could find Annabel, to ask her and my brother and Caroline over to the Jays' house for drinks. And she came in here from the terrace and she did find Annabel, lying dead on the floor. She must have collapsed and died there only a very short time before Leslie came in. And seeing her, the horrible scheme for killing Caroline came into her mind. I suppose she hated her because she believed my brother was in love with her. I don't know about that, but I assume that was her motive. And she knew where there was a gun and she thought that if she left it beside Annabel's body she would naturally be thought to be guilty, which she would have been if Leslie hadn't made the mistake of cleaning all the fingerprints off the gun.'

'But it was the sight of Annabel lying there dead that

killed Caroline, was it?' Gavin said. 'And Nigel said there was no danger from the dead.'

'It may interest you to know that Mr Cleaver and Miss Astor were married in Oxford a fortnight ago,' Frost said, 'so your guess as to the motive of the murder, if your theory should prove to be right, is possibly correct. But of course a theory is only a theory. Finding proof may be another matter.'

'I should have thought the way she dashed away when we put this to her,' Helena said, 'comes very near to being a proof.'

'It doesn't!' Marion cried. 'She was frightened, that's all! She was terrified by your outrageous accusations.'

'She wouldn't have been if she'd been innocent,' Helena said. 'We put it to her very quietly and reasonably, but a mixture of Barbara's practical intelligence and my imagination was too much for her. I do hope Barbara's wrong about that cliff she mentioned. She doesn't mean to be unkind, but she can be very cold-blooded sometimes. She doesn't understand other people's feelings. Of course I knew from the first that Nigel had been in love with Caroline, even though I didn't know it had gone as far as marriage. And Leslie killed him, I suppose, partly because of the pain of being rejected, but also, of course, because he knew she was guilty.'

'But how did she expect to get away from the house after killing Miss Astor, if you're right?' Frost asked.

'I think she'd have rung up the police herself,' Barbara said, 'and told them she'd found things as they were. Jerome Halliday would have been a convenient scapegoat.'

'No,' Gavin said. 'She didn't see him arrive. If she had, the murder wouldn't have happened. She must have done it already when he came. But I don't believe Nigel meant to accuse her. To go by what he said just before he died, he believed he was to blame for what she'd done. He'd treated her pretty abominably and he knew it.'

There was a sudden loud knock on the front door.

However, there had been no sound of cars arriving or of men's voices outside, so it did not seem probable that this could be the other police whom Frost was expecting, and when he opened the door it was Desmond Jay who stood there.

'Is my wife here?' he asked. 'She left a note for me at the house to tell me she and my daughter were coming here.'

'Your wife is here,' Frost said.

Marion leapt out of her chair and as her husband came into the room threw herself into his arms.

'She's gone, Des!' she moaned. 'They've been saying fearful things about her and she's gone!'

'She has?' he said. 'How long ago?'

His tone was curiously calm, but it seemed to Gavin that he was taking care not to meet the eyes of any of the Cleavers in the room. So he had had his suspicions of his daughter before now, Gavin thought, though it was natural enough that he should have kept them to himself.

'Ten minutes, quarter of an hour ago, I don't know,' Marion answered. 'Oh, what are we going to do?'

Jay turned to Frost. 'Can you tell me what's been happening? All I know about it is the note my wife left behind in the house.'

Birefly Frost told him of Nigel's death and then, after a moment, when it seemed he was uncertain of how much more he should say, he added a few sentences about what Barbara and Helena had had to say about Leslie's guilt.

Jay made no response to that, but then, with an arm round Marion, he said, 'Is there any reason why we shouldn't go home, Mr Frost? You seem to have enough people here and you'll know where to find us.'

'That's right,' Frost said. 'I should go.'

'Thank you.'

'But do you know,' Marion said, with her face half-hidden against her husband's shoulder, 'for a time I was afraid it was you, I really was?'

'In a way, I wish you'd been right,' Jay said sombrely. 'Come along.'

Still very careful not to look into the faces of Gavin or either of his sisters, Desmond Jay guided Marion out of the room.

The front door had only just clanged shut behind them when there was a sound of cars being driven up to it and of voices in the courtyard and Frost opened the door to let in his reinforcements.

Almost at once he suggested to Gavin and the two women that they should go to the cottage and wait there until he required to question them further. They walked over to the cottage in silence and as soon as they were there Barbara made coffee and Helena helped herself to whisky.

'Do you know, I've never been drunk in my life,' she said, 'but it's what I should like to be now. Couldn't we all sit down together and drink till we're really drunk? Then if that man comes to question us he'll see there really isn't any point in bothering us. We couldn't be held responsible for what we said.'

It seemed to Gavin that there was a good deal to be said in favour of this scheme, but Barbara refused to cooperate and when it came to the point Gavin found that at that time in the morning he preferred coffee to whisky. The three of them waited for a long time but Frost did not appear and presently there was a sound of cars being driven away, lights in the windows of the house disappeared and a strange quiet descended on the place.

So evidently Frost had no more questions to ask that night, or rather that morning, for by the time that Barbara and Helena decided to go up to bed the soft, eerie light that comes before dawn was beginning to appear in the sky. Helena, Gavin thought, really was mildly drunk by then. She kept asserting, to Barbara's irritation, that it had been her sensitivity to atmosphere that had explained how Leslie had managed to cross the courtyard, apparently invisibly, while Barbara grunted that it had been only common sense. They left Gavin feeling a little ashamed that he had not thought of the explanation himself. Perhaps after all, he thought, in spite of their eccentricities, both of his sisters were a little cleverer than he was.

He did not go to bed at all, but sat in the easy chair, dropping off into an occasional cat-nap, but not truly sleeping, though in one of these, which actually lasted only a few minutes he had a curiously vivid dream that he was in some great shadowy building which might have been a cathedral or perhaps a railway station, or perhaps even an enormously enlarged hall of the Cantlewell Museum in Tolcaster, and that Mrs Nevin had arrived there on her bicycle, her fair curls bobbing on top of her head, and told him that she did not intend to work for Nigel and Annabel any more because where they were there would be too much talk. It wouldn't be nice and quiet as it used to be, besides, they wouldn't need her. She complained that after having worked for them for twelve years they were treating her very inconsiderately, but said she supposed they might like a change. 'Wouldn't you like a change, Mr Cleaver?' she said distinctly only just before he woke up. 'You've a bit of money now, Mr Cleaver. Wouldn't you like a change?'

His first clear feeling as she vanished was that the last thing in life that he wanted then was change. He desperately wanted the tried, the trusted, the familiar. He longed to be at home again in the security of Stillborough.

But it was a little while before he could return to it. On the nine o'clock news, in time for which Barbara and Helena had come down sleepily from their rooms to drink more coffee and eat toast and marmalade, they heard that with relation to the death of the actress, Caroline Astor, found dead in her sister's house on Saturday morning, a woman was helping the police with their inquiries. Frost came to the cottage later in the morning and confirmed that it was Leslie Jay who had been arrested and would shortly be charged with murder, and that as it had been Gavin who had found the bodies of both Caroline and Nigel, his presence would be required at the court hearing. Frost told him that the Wellingtons that Leslie had been wearing when she was found had certainly made the footprints in the dining-room. That also was something on which his evidence would be wanted. But Barbara and Helena were allowed to go home. They shared a taxi to the station, though by the time that they got into it they were arguing as to whether they should catch the next train to London, which happened to be a slow one, or wait for the next fast one. There was no more talk of their running a guest-house together in Upthorn. The house and the cottage would eventually be put on the market.

When they had gone Gavin set off for a walk by himself on the downs. He was sure that he would never come back to see the low green hills again, but for the moment their emptiness and quiet, with the wide landscape that he could see when he reached the summit, the villages, the copses, the meadows and the occasional glint of a stream, seemed kindly and soothing. For a few minutes at a time he found it almost possible to forget what had been happening in the valley below him during the last few days. Those moments never lasted for long, but at least they were something for which to be grateful.